Kung Fu Princess 2

In Gold and Jade

KUNG FU PRINCESS 2

IN GOLD AND JADE

WRITTEN BY PAMELA WALKER

GROSSET & DUNLAP
A PARACHUTE PRESS BOOK

PARACHUTE PRESS

GROSSET & DUNLAP
Published by the Penguin Group
Penguin Group (USA) Inc., 375 Hudson Street, New York, New York 10014, U.S.A.
Penguin Group (Canada), 90 Eglinton Avenue East, Suite 700, Toronto, Ontario,
Canada M4P 2Y3 (a division of Pearson Penguin Canada Inc.)
Penguin Books Ltd, 80 Strand, London WC2R 0RL, England
Penguin Ireland, 25 St Stephen's Green, Dublin 2, Ireland
(a division of Penguin Books Ltd)
Penguin Group (Australia), 250 Camberwell Road, Camberwell, Victoria 3124,
Australia (a division of Pearson Australia Group Pty Ltd)
Penguin Books India Pvt Ltd, 11 Community Centre, Panchsheel Park,
New Delhi -110 017, India
Penguin Group (NZ), Cnr Airborne and Rosedale Roads, Albany, Auckland 1310,
New Zealand (a division of Pearson New Zealand Ltd)
Penguin Books (South Africa) (Pty) Ltd, 24 Sturdee Avenue, Rosebank,
Johannesburg 2196, South Africa
Penguin Books Ltd, Registered Offices:
80 Strand, London WC2R 0RL, England

Cover photograph by David Mager/Pearson Learning Group

Library of Congress Control Number: 2006013229

ISBN 0-448-44140-3   10 9 8 7 6 5 4 3 2 1

The Prophecy

A daughter of light,

Blood of Ng Mui and Yim Wing Chun,

Will be born into the power of her ancestors,

Born to finish the battles they began.

In her fourteenth year her destiny will unfold:

Through five gold coins, each death or strength.

Her ancestors' enemies will seek her,

The demons and ghosts will gather,

But in gold and jade, she will find her gifts,

And the veil of secrets will open to her.

Prologue

The ancient prophecy began to unfold on Cassidy Chen's fourteenth birthday, when a strange man appeared out of nowhere and gave her a gift of five ancient Chinese coins. He quietly disappeared into the foggy morning, but his visit had forever changed Cassidy's life.

That night Cassidy dreamed of the two legendary women warriors Ng Mui and Wing Chun. *"Much has been given to you, Mingmei,"* they told Cassidy, calling her by her Chinese name, *"and much is expected."*

Cassidy learned that five evil spirits, imprisoned in the ancient coins for more than three hundred years, had now been released. *"These spirits are restless and want revenge, Mingmei. As you are of our blood, they will try to destroy you."*

In the following days, Cassidy became the victim of bizarre accidents and unexplainable illness. On a night when Cassidy was at her weakest, she came face-to-face with unthinkable evil—a flying snake demon, just like the one pictured in the first coin. After a terrifying battle, Cassidy defeated the snake demon with an antique Chinese sword. Cassidy's victory earned her a gift from the spirits of her ancestors—*the ability to heal quickly.*

With help from a friend, Cassidy discovered that the second coin represented an ancient demon known as the plague ghost. This demon brought unnatural weather—torrential rain, wind, and unrelenting thunderstorms—to Seattle. In a spectacular fight to the death, Cassidy defeated the ancient demon using kung fu skills learned from Master Lau, her beloved teacher. For defeating the plague ghost, Cassidy received *the gift of second sight—of seeing spirits.*

Cassidy was amazed that she had actually defeated *two* demons—but this wasn't the life she wanted. She longed to return to the life of a normal fourteen-year-old girl.

Then Cassidy made an unusual discovery. The man who gave her the coins looked exactly like her long-gone grandfather! The startling news gave her the first stirrings of hope that she might one day understand what was happening—yet for now, it raised even more questions. *Did my grandfather's ghost give me the coins? Or is my grandfather actually alive?*

Cassidy knew now that she couldn't run from or change her destiny. She *had* to find answers to her many questions—*Why was I given the coins? How is my grandfather involved? Who is the ally promised by my ancestors?* And the most terrifying question of all—*What demon will I have to face next?*

Three coins remain . . . The story continues . . .

❀ Chapter One

Cassidy Chen looked out over the fog-shrouded lake and watched breathlessly as the mist began to shift and change. First one, then two, then dozens, and possibly even *hundreds* of illuminated figures formed out of the fog that reflected the warm golden light of the rising sun. Cassidy felt her breath quicken as she watched the number of spirits continue to grow. They looked like transparent watercolor sketches against the cold January sky.

The sight of these ghostlike men and women made Cassidy's pulse race. Her fighting instincts ramped up, and her brain readied itself to make the split-second decision to fight—or flee. She glanced around for a way out, a place to run if she had to. But as she took a moment to steady herself, the spirits began to look familiar to her. And she was able to sense a strong connection to them.

One of the spirits, a tall woman in a long, shimmering dress, walked toward Cassidy. As she moved, the mist parted and turned luminous shades of green and blue around her, reflecting the rich colors of her dress. Her reddish hair had a fiery brilliance that sparked with pinpoints of light, and her jade green eyes radiated kindness.

"You're my great-grandmother," Cassidy said, her heart warming as the woman smiled at her. She recognized the beautiful spirit who had appeared in her room the night she received the gift of second sight, of *seeing* spirits.

"*Look around,*" Cassidy's great-grandmother said, her Irish accent lilting like golden bells.

Cassidy took in her surroundings. A shimmering throng of ghostlike creatures stood shoulder to shoulder across the entire surface of the lake. Irish ancestors from her mother's side and Chinese ancestors from her father's side. The light that shone from each spirit was as pure and golden as the sunlight that spilled over them. Cassidy felt the exquisite joy of their love deep within her, and its force took her breath away.

"*Your life is made up of all these lives,*" her great-grandmother said as she opened her arms wide. "*These* are your ancestors, my daughter. You are here now because we were here before you. We are all bound together like pieces of a quilt. Each individual piece is beautiful and strong—but made even more beautiful and stronger by our connections to each other."

Cassidy's heart swelled as she listened to her great-grandmother's words. She *felt* their concern for her and was comforted by it.

"We are delighted that our presence brings you comfort, dear one—but there is another reason we came to you on this glorious morning. Your destiny is like this path. It is both where you have been and where you are going. You've defeated two powerful demons—but there are more."

Cassidy's legs suddenly went weak. Her great-grandmother wasn't just making a friendly visit. She was here to tell Cassidy to start preparing herself. The next demon could soon be coming after her. She had been waiting to receive a message like this for a while now—ever since she defeated the last demon. There were still three remaining demons—each represented by one of the three remaining coins.

"The third coin," she said, her voice trembling. "Can you tell me what it is? What will happen? When?"

The kind spirit shook her head. *"I can only tell you that a true warrior is always prepared, always ready for what is to come. You must be strong, my child. Demons wait for you in the shadowy darkness of the world—and of the mind."*

🌼 Chapter Two

"What about these?" Cassidy put on a pair of black cat's-eye sunglasses studded with tiny green rhinestones.

Eliza Clifford, Cassidy's best friend, nodded her approval. "Definitely," she said. "But how much?"

Cassidy checked the price tag. "Two dollars."

"Score!" Eliza cried. "I bet my mom can sell them for twenty, maybe even thirty."

It was Saturday, and Cassidy and Eliza were trolling the thrift shops that lined the perimeter of Pike Place Market. Eliza's mom had promised the girls a percentage of the profits for anything they found that she could resell in her online auction business. So far they had bought a zebra-striped handbag with black lacquer handles, a psychedelic miniskirt, and a vintage pair of acid green Hush Puppies.

"Want to go to Future?" Eliza asked Cassidy as they waited for the salesclerk to ring up the rhinestone-studded glasses. "They're pretty cheap, and my mom's found amazing stuff in there."

"Might want to try Go-Go's," the salesclerk told them as she slid the glasses into a shopping bag. "They're having some kind of huge, down-to-the-bare-walls sale."

As they walked down the sidewalk, Eliza told Cassidy that her mother had started talking again about moving to Phoenix.

"I thought she was dating that Patrick guy now and had kind of changed her mind about moving," Cassidy said.

"Dropped him," Eliza told her. "Said that he smelled like patchouli all the time and it was affecting her allergies."

"That's too bad," Cassidy said.

"The whole thing's seriously messed up," Eliza said disgustedly. "I just don't think she understands how much I don't want to leave Seattle. But what can I do to make her *get* it, you know? How can I get her attention?"

It was a good question, but Cassidy didn't have the answer.

"Hey, there's Go-Go's," Eliza said, pointing across the street and dropping for now the puzzling question of how to get her point across to her mother.

As they walked toward Go-Go's, Cassidy had to stop and pull the hem of her jeans out of the top of her shoe, where it had gotten caught. "These are too short!" she said, shaking her foot and pulling at the flared leg of her jeans.

"So buy some new ones," Eliza said. "You're always working at your mom's preschool. She does *pay* you, doesn't she?"

"Sometimes," Cassidy said. "Not enough for the kind of jeans I want, though."

"Let's check out VibeBuy later," Eliza said. "I love their clothes."

Just before reaching the turquoise storefront of Go-Go's, the girls passed the frosted-glass door of the Chinese Tiger Antiques and Gifts. Cassidy remembered the day, not long after her birthday, when she brought the five ancient coins into the store to see if the owner knew anything about them. He said they were real gold, but he didn't want to buy them. The owner thought they had bad chi, and he didn't even want them in his store.

"I think I'll run in here a minute," Cassidy told Eliza. "Wanna come with?"

Eliza looked at the door of the Chinese Tiger and shook her head. "I don't want to miss the sale at Go-Go's," she said. "I'll catch up with you later."

Cassidy had been thinking about buying a shrine ever since James Tang, the five-times-gorgeous hottie from her Wing Chun class, had suggested that she set one up and ask for her ancestors' help in fighting the demons. And now that the third coin was about to unleash its demon, she needed all the help she could get. Besides, if James really was her ally—her ancestors had promised that she would find one—then she figured she should listen to him. But Cassidy had to be honest with herself. The other reason she wanted to buy a shrine was so that she could tell James about it at Wing Chun on Wednesday. *Then maybe he'll want to come over and see it.*

Cassidy stepped through the door of the cramped Chinese Tiger. The same pale yellow bulbs hung from the ceiling. The amber glow shed by the bulbs created weak pools of light and thick, peculiar shadows.

She didn't see the owner anywhere. The massive green desk was against the wall, and it was piled high with papers and small boxes, but this time the chair was empty.

An antique broadsword hung against the brick wall, and it caught Cassidy's eye. It was a beautiful sword—not as beautiful as the *nandao* that James had with him the night she killed the snake demon—but still, the hilt was a heavy silver engraved with a delicate tracery of feathers and leaves. The brightly polished blade looked razor sharp and absolutely deadly against the dark wall. Was it just her imagination, or could she actually feel how it would rest in her hands—the weight of it, the perfect balance?

"A warrior's sword," she heard a man say behind her. Cassidy turned, and there was the shopkeeper, his gold-framed eyeglasses halfway down his nose as they had been the first time she met him. The look on his face left no doubt that he remembered her as the girl with the five coins—the five *bad chi* coins.

"Don't worry," Cassidy said, holding up empty hands. "I don't have them with me today."

He lowered his voice as if he were afraid to even speak about them. "Did you . . . get rid of them?"

"No," she said. "I still have them."

He raised an eyebrow. "Did you find out anything about them?"

Cassidy shrugged. She wasn't sure she wanted to say anything to this stranger.

He crossed his arms over his chest and smirked. "You did, didn't you?"

"Not *bad*!" Cassidy protested. "The coins were made by warriors a long time ago. Whenever they defeated a powerful enemy, they had a coin made—to celebrate."

He shook his head. "I don't know about celebrating. Those were serious bad chi."

Cassidy wanted to get off the subject of the coins. "Do you have any shrines?"

The man looked surprised. "Shrines?" he

repeated. Cassidy thought he looked sort of impressed. "An honorable thing to purchase."

He directed Cassidy to a case at the front of the store. She pointed to a small but beautifully carved mahogany shrine with inlays of gold and jade. "That's really nice," she said.

"Notice that the sides are hinged," he said, picking it up and folding the two smaller panels into the larger middle one. "This was known as the warrior's shrine. It could be folded small and tucked into a warrior's pack during travel."

Cassidy examined the smooth, dark wood and the ornately carved branches and leaves that connected the three panels.

"The warrior gathered strength by meditating on the intricate pattern of the leaves," the shopkeeper went on. "The jade represented the power necessary to fight, and the gold reminded the warrior to keep a pure heart even in the midst of battle."

Cassidy ran her fingertips over the gold inlays, which felt warm to the touch. Then she traced the jade, which felt cool. *Opposites,* she thought. *Yin and yang. Dark and light. Warm and cool.* "I love it," she said. "But I'm positive I can't afford it. It must be an antique, and it's so . . . so beautiful."

With disappointment, Cassidy handed the shrine back to the shopkeeper. He looked at the shrine and then back at Cassidy. "You're lucky," he said. "We're having a sale today. With the discount, the shrine will be five dollars."

Cassidy couldn't believe what she'd just heard. "Five dollars? The shrine must be worth much more than that."

"It's difficult to put an exact price on a shrine," he told her. "But as I said, we're having a sale."

"Did I hear the word 'sale'?" Eliza said, stepping in through the door. "That's my favorite word." She dropped a Go-Go shopping bag beside the door and joined Cassidy at the counter, where the shopkeeper was wrapping the shrine in tissue paper.

"Whatcha buying?" Eliza asked.

"Huh? Oh..." Cassidy fumbled in her backpack for her money and paid the shopkeeper. He smiled at her and said, "Your ancestors will be very pleased that you honor them with such a beautiful shrine."

"Shrine?" Eliza repeated.

The shopkeeper laughed. "A warrior shrine for a true warrior," he said with a wink. "Perhaps it will help you handle those coins."

Cassidy cringed. Why did Eliza have to come into the store? "Thanks," she told him, taking the little shopping bag. "We've got to go." *Before you say anything else in front of Eliza!*

"Come back anytime," he called after her.

Outside, Cassidy turned to face Eliza, who didn't look very happy.

Not very happy at all.

Chapter Three

"*Warrior shrine?*" Eliza asked with a puzzled look on her face. "For coins?"

"I don't know what that was all about," Cassidy said, avoiding Eliza's gaze.

The two girls had been friends for a long time, and it was almost impossible for Cassidy to lie to Eliza. But she had lied—or at least, she hadn't been completely honest about the strange, even *supernatural* things that had been happening to her since she was given the coins on her fourteenth birthday.

"Let's see," Eliza said, cocking her head. "This guy who runs an old antique-y, weirdish sort of store—

says a *warrior* shrine is perfect for you. The Cassidy I know might have a shrine to her hottie friend James. But a *warrior* shrine?"

Cassidy could tell that her friend wasn't about to give up. Cassidy could say that the guy was just nuts and she didn't know what he was talking about. And Eliza *might* accept this and drop it, and they would go on to the next thrift shop to look for retro sweatshirts. And it probably wouldn't come up again . . . at least, not until the next strange thing happened. And the way things were going, that could be five minutes from now.

Or . . . Cassidy could finally tell Eliza the truth. Would Eliza even believe her? Cassidy couldn't be sure. The only thing she knew was that she didn't want to lie to her best friend anymore.

"Okay," Cassidy said, lowering her voice. "I think I need to tell you about some things that have been going on." She glanced around to be sure no one would be able to overhear her. "Some . . . well, sort of bizarre, even sort of *unbelievable* things."

"Cass, you're scaring me," Eliza said, her eyes widening. "You're not involved in some kind of witch coven or cult, are you?"

Cassidy laughed, secretly wondering if Eliza would think the actual truth was any weirder. "Where do you even come up with ideas like that? You do know that you're seriously kind of warped?"

Eliza grinned. "Yeah, I'm aware of that. It's

why you love me, though. I really think it's probably my best feature—my warped mind, that is."

"Actually, your pink hair is probably your best feature."

"Come on, tell me what's going on, Cass," Eliza said, her voice serious again. "When you say *bizarre things*, you mean *what* exactly?"

Cassidy took a deep breath and looked straight at Eliza. *Can I do this?* she asked herself. *Once I tell her, I can't go back. Will she think I'm making it up?* Then a worse thought occurred to her. *Maybe she'll think I'm just crazy.*

Cassidy waited for a mom pushing a stroller to pass them. "Remember those coins I got for my birthday?" Cassidy began. "From the stranger?"

"Yeah, some kind of Chinese coins, right?" Eliza nodded toward the Chinese Tiger. "And that guy in the store told you they were dangerous or haunted or something, right? He wouldn't buy them."

"Yeah, well, they are . . . kind of bad, I mean," Cassidy said, and cringed at the way it sounded. "Not the coins, exactly, but what they represent."

Eliza frowned and shook her head. "Okay, I'm trying to understand, but I'm not getting it. Why don't you just say it? Whatever it is, just say it."

Cassidy saw now that this would be even harder than she'd imagined. *How can you make somebody believe such . . . such unbelievable stuff?*

"Remember right after my birthday when I

got the coins, I was sick for a while and missed some school?" Cassidy asked.

"Sure," Eliza said, nodding. "Your mom took you to Patrick Healy—the New Agey guy my mom dated. I remember."

"Well, he asked me if I'd been . . ." Cassidy wondered if she could actually say the word. It would sound so ridiculous to say it out loud on an ordinary Saturday in Seattle.

"Cursed," Cassidy said at last. "Patrick asked me if I'd been *cursed*."

"Right," Eliza said. "Your mom was really upset and told my mom all about it. Your mom said going to him had been a complete waste of time and she thought he was a quack." She gave an irritated little snort. "Of course that didn't stop *my* mom from dating him." She rolled her eyes, then caught Cassidy's expression. "Oh, sorry. I'm rambling. Totally focused now. So what does Patrick have to do with the coins?"

"Well, actually, he was right. I *was* cursed."

"Is this supposed to be, like, a joke or something?" Eliza asked with a laugh. "How could you be *cursed*?"

Cassidy prayed that her friend would really hear her, would *accept* what she said, but she also knew that this might be too much to ask. "It was a poison sickness, and it was caused by a . . . a . . . demon," she managed to stammer out.

Eliza stared at her, blinking. "Come on, Cass,"

Eliza said finally. Cassidy was pretty sure Eliza was struggling to not laugh. "*Poison sickness? Demon?*"

"Maybe I shouldn't have said anything." Cassidy was beginning to regret her decision.

"Oookay, well, you seem fine now," Eliza said.

Cassidy swallowed. "That's because I . . . I killed it," she said. She watched Eliza's face, hoping to see some understanding—some *acceptance* of what she was saying.

"You *killed* it? Do you even hear what you're saying, Cass?" Eliza asked, her voice rising in disbelief and frustration.

A couple passing by glanced over at Eliza, and Cassidy cringed. "Not so loud," Cassidy whispered.

"You don't even like to step on bugs," Eliza said in a slightly lower voice. "And you're telling me you *killed* some *demon* or something!"

"Yeah, Eliza, I killed it in the woods the night of Tamika's Halloween party," Cassidy said, really wishing now that she could take it all back. It seemed every sentence she uttered was more bizarre than the one before. She couldn't blame Eliza for not believing her. If the tables were turned, she wasn't sure whether she'd believe herself, either.

For a moment Eliza didn't say anything. She looked across the street at a small, tree-lined park. Usually it was bustling with kids climbing on the stone turtle statues in the center. Today, probably because of a brisk February chill in the air, the park was empty.

"Okay, let's go hang with the turtles. I think I need to sit down to hear the rest of this. Because what I've heard so far still doesn't make a lot of sense."

So Cassidy and Eliza climbed onto the back of a large stone turtle and faced each other. And Cassidy told Eliza about the ancient coins and the visions of her ancestors and the demons. And when she finished talking, she watched Eliza sit still, in silence.

She thinks I'm crazy, Cassidy thought. *She thinks I've totally lost my mind.*

"Okay, here's what I think. Maybe when you were sick, it was like a virus or something," Eliza offered. "I mean you had a fever, maybe it gave you bad dreams. And dreams can seem really real, right? I mean, take a look at your dream journal—"

"No, Eliza," Cassidy said firmly, determined now to make Eliza believe her. "It all happened, just like I said."

"But Cassidy, there's no way any of this stuff really happened!" Eliza said. "What you just told me is like . . . like a movie. Maybe that's it! You've watched too many of those kung fu movies and you sort of got it all mixed up."

"It's *not* a movie, Eliza," Cassidy snapped, then took a deep breath to calm down. She didn't want to say anything she might regret. "Look, I didn't have to tell you any of this, okay? If you want to forget everything I've just said, that's fine."

"I don't want—I mean, I *can't* forget it, Cassidy,"

Eliza said, her words softer now. "This is just too . . ."

"I know," Cassidy said. "It's too *everything*—too unbelievable, too crazy, too scary."

"All right, I'm trying to be open-minded here, but help me," Eliza said. "So are you saying that the night you and James came out of the park at Tamika's party, you'd just killed the *demon*?" Eliza's voice cracked on the last word.

"Yes," Cassidy said. "It almost strangled me."

Eliza winced. Then she frowned. "And that time during all the rain when I thought I saw you fighting some old man under the bridge, that was actually some *other* kind of demon?"

"The plague ghost," Cassidy said. "He sort of looked like an old man, but he was really powerful. He almost drowned me. Actually, he almost wiped out all of Seattle."

Eliza ran a hand through her pink hair. "Cassidy, do you even hear what you're saying? I mean, if these things really exist—or existed—they tried to *kill* you! And you're just sitting here, as if it's all totally normal!"

"I don't have much of a choice," Cassidy said.

"I don't buy it." Eliza shook her head. "Why don't you just make it all stop? Get rid of the coins and go back to a normal life. Forget all this crazy stuff about demons and curses." She took a deep breath. "You said there are, what—like three more coins? So just throw them away and forget you ever saw them."

"That's just it. I don't think I can," Cassidy said. "Eliza, I don't understand most of this destiny stuff, but I do know I'm caught in something really old. And really big. And the only thing I can do is be ready to fight whatever's coming next." She felt the weight of the shrine in the red and gold bag from the Chinese Tiger. *A warrior's shrine—to take into battle.*

"God, Cass." Eliza rubbed her forehead as if her brain hurt, trying to take in all the information. "This all sounds lethal. Maybe your parents could . . ." There was a pause while Eliza tried to figure out what to say next.

"Exactly," Cassidy said. "My parents could do—*what*? That's one of the reasons I haven't told them. I *know* they'd want to do something, and I really don't think there's anything they can do. The time may come when I have to tell them, but right now, I guess it's my *ancestors* who are giving me advice—not that I always understand it."

Eliza seemed to be out of questions and out of suggestions. She looked pale—even the chilly air couldn't put color in her face. "I'm trying to believe you, Cassidy," she said. "But you've gotta admit that it all sounds . . ."

"I know how it sounds," Cassidy said. "But I know what I've seen, Eliza, and I know what's already happened. The problem is that I don't know what's going to happen *next.*"

Chapter Four

The sun had turned the sky a silvery pink, and Cassidy glanced at her watch. "I've gotta go home," she said. "We're going out to dinner. My mom will kill me if I'm late."

"Yeah, me too," Eliza said.

"I'm glad I got it all out in the open, Eliza. I mean, I hope that you . . . don't mind," Cassidy said, wondering if things would be awkward between them now. *Maybe I should have just kept my mouth shut*, she thought.

Eliza gave a helpless shrug. "Honestly, Cass, I don't know what I feel right now. I guess it'll take a while for it all to sink in."

"I know," Cassidy said. "But I'm glad I told you."

"Me too. I *think*," Eliza said with a half smile.

The girls walked silently out of the park under trees that were as bare as dark skeletons.

They crossed the street and headed for the metro transit stop at Pioneer Square. Eliza let out a little gasp and grabbed Cassidy's arm. "Did you see that?" Eliza asked. "That dog just ran into the traffic."

Cassidy looked across the sea of cars but didn't see anything. "You think it was hit?"

"I don't know, but maybe we should check," Eliza said. When the light turned green, the girls ran across the street, looking for a sign of a dog.

Eliza pointed to an opening between two buildings. "Maybe he ran in there," she said. They scurried to the entrance of the narrow and twisted alley. "I don't see anything, do you?" she asked, peering down the length of the dark alley.

"No," Cassidy said. "And I really don't want to walk through there, either. It reeks." A sour garbage smell hung heavy in the air, and the ground was dark and slick around the trash cans and Dumpsters.

"I just hope the dog's not in there, hurt or scared, you know?" Eliza said.

"We'd hear whimpering or something if it were hurt," Cassidy said. "It must not have been hit."

"I guess you're right," Eliza conceded, turning.

"Let's get going. It's gross in there." She started to head back up the street.

But at that moment Cassidy saw something. An animal ran out from behind a large trash can near the end of the alley. It paused and looked back down the dark passage toward Cassidy and Eliza, opening its mouth wide in . . . *In what? A grin? A sneer?*

Cassidy took one step toward the alley. The animal turned its head slightly and then nodded, as if to say, *Come with me.* Its eyes glittered, catching the reflection of a streetlight on the corner. Its gray coat was shaggy, and Cassidy saw that its front feet ended in yellowish claws. With one last nod, it turned and disappeared into the alley's inky shadows.

Too weird, Cassidy thought. "Did you just see that?" she asked, feeling very unsettled.

Eliza stopped and turned around. "Was it the dog? Is it hurt?" She walked back toward Cassidy.

"I don't think it was hurt. I'm not even sure it was a dog." Cassidy said. She glanced back into the alley. "It kind of looked like a small wolf or a fox."

"In the middle of the city?" Eliza scoffed. "Only if it escaped from the zoo."

But if it wasn't a dog, then what was it? Cassidy wondered, peering into the darkness of the alley.

Whatever the thing was, Cassidy decided, she couldn't shake the feeling that it had stopped and deliberately *looked* at them. *As if it knows who we are.*

As if it wanted us to follow.

🏵 *Chapter Five*

When Cassidy got home, she found her mother sitting at the dining room table cutting out red and pink construction-paper hearts. "Only twenty more to go," Wendy Chen said. "Wanna help me cut out valentines for the Happy Bunny?"

"Sure, Mom," Cassidy said. "How much does this job pay, like a dollar a heart or something?"

"Actually, it pays for your dinner tonight—how about that?"

"Dinner's fine, but I could really use some cash." Cassidy sighed. "I kind of need some new jeans."

Wendy looked up from her snipping and pointed

with her scissors toward the package that Cassidy had placed on the end of the table. "Looks like you had enough money to buy something there," she said.

Cassidy took the shrine out of the bag. She peeled the tissue paper away from the delicately carved dark wood and placed it in front of her mom. Cassidy lifted the brass clasp and opened up the panels.

"Oh, Cassidy, that's beautiful," her mother said, putting down her scissors and a red paper heart. "Is it an antique?"

"I think so," Cassidy said. "I got it at this shop called the Chinese Tiger. It's a warrior's shrine—that's why it's so small and it folds up like this. So the warrior could take it with him when he went into battle."

Wendy picked up the shrine and touched the gold and jade inlay. "Don't tell me you're going to let Sarah Clifford sell this on eBay."

"No, actually I bought it for myself," Cassidy said. "I saw it and I just really liked it. I got a good deal on it, too."

Wendy turned the shrine over and frowned. "But how could you afford this, honey?"

"It was just five dollars, Mom," Cassidy said. "The guy was having a sale."

Wendy's eyebrows raised, and she turned the shrine upside down. Cassidy now noticed a tiny white sticker on the bottom. "Then that was some sale," Wendy said. "Because according to the sticker, this shrine costs three hundred dollars."

Cassidy was shocked to hear this. She'd had no idea that the guy was giving her such a break. But given how wigged out he was by the coins, it made sense. He probably realized that Cassidy needed the shrine more than he needed the two hundred and ninety-five dollars.

ම ම ම ම ම

After the Chens returned from dinner that evening, Cassidy decided to set up the shrine in her room. She wasn't sure of the best place for it and tried it out on her window ledge, her computer desk, and her dresser. Finally she settled on her nightstand. She opened the three panels and ran her fingers along the polished wood, the gold leaves, and jade petals. She marveled at how compact it was. With the three panels opened, it was no larger than a small laptop.

Now, what am I supposed to put in front of it? she wondered. She scanned her room and saw that Monty, her ginger cat, had come into the room and was sitting on the foot of the bed, watching her with interest. "That's right, Monty, I don't know what I'm doing, okay?" Monty meowed and then swiped the air with his paw as if to say, *Of course you don't, but I'm sure that won't stop you from trying.*

So what kinds of things would honor my ancestors? She opened a dresser drawer and took out a pink box. Inside was a small dog carved from jade. It was a good-luck charm that her dad had given Cassidy for her fourteenth birthday. "You were born in the year of the dog—this symbol is good luck for you," he had told her. "It's also a connection to your Chinese heritage."

Cassidy remembered that the shopkeeper at the Chinese Tiger had told her that jade represented the power necessary to fight. *That's good enough for me,* Cassidy thought. She placed the green jade dog charm in front of the shrine.

Next she pulled out an old tortoiseshell comb that her mother had given her. It had once belonged to her great-grandmother—the beautiful, red-haired woman who had appeared to Cassidy as a spirit. As Cassidy placed the comb in front of the shrine, she remembered her great-grandmother's words that morning at the lake. *"Demons wait for you in the shadowy darkness of the world—and of the mind."* Cassidy shuddered. The words had clearly been a warning—but of what?

"Hey, Cass." Her father was standing in her doorway. "I wasn't sure if you were still up."

"Come in," Cassidy called. "I'm kind of working on this shrine—like I even know what I'm doing."

Simon grinned. "Well, I happen to think this is a great thing. I'm really glad you're taking such an interest in your family history and in your culture. Especially since your mother and I haven't been all that connected to our past."

Cassidy wondered what her dad would say if

she told him that her ancestors had visited her in spirit form and making this shrine was a way to honor them and thank them for their help.

Instead she shrugged. "I saw this shrine and I just thought it was so . . . beautiful, you know? I mean, I don't know much about setting one up or what should be included."

Simon looked at the jade dog and the comb that Cassidy had placed in front of the shrine.

"Well, I think some people use a candle or incense—but you know your mother will have a fit if you leave candles or incense burning in here."

"Candles and incense. Cool." She grinned at her dad. "I know, I know. I *promise* I'll always put them out before I leave."

"What about a photograph?" Simon suggested. "I've been scanning some of those old photos from the albums your mother found."

"Do you have that picture of your father?" Cassidy asked him. "The one in front of the bridge?"

Cassidy's grandfather had died when Simon was just a young man, long before Cassidy was born. She had never known what he'd looked like until recently, when Simon showed her a picture. Cassidy was startled to see how much he looked like the old man who had given her the coins on her birthday. They even both had the same unusual white streak in their hair.

"I haven't scanned that one yet, but remind

me and I'll get it for you tomorrow," Simon told her. "Right now, I'm thinking about turning in. It's late."

"Yeah, me too," she said. "I'll finish the shrine tomorrow."

"My mother had a shrine in the kitchen," her father said. "She used to send up prayers to our ancestors." He shook his head ruefully. "I don't even have any idea who our ancestors are."

I do, Cassidy thought. *You wouldn't believe how clear an idea of them I have.*

As Simon left the room, Cassidy heard their neighbor's dog bark outside her window. The noise frightened Monty, who jumped from the end of the bed onto Cassidy's dresser. "It's okay, Monty," Cassidy said, rubbing her cat's furry yellow head. "It's just that dumb dog next door."

She remembered the animal in the alley that she and Eliza had seen earlier that day. *That was* definitely *not a dog. But could it have been a fox?*

Cassidy pulled a chair over to her closet to get the box of coins that she kept on the top shelf. The coins seemed to agitate Monty, so Cassidy had started keeping them out of the cat's sight.

As she took the coins from the shelf, she heard a strange growl. She looked over at Monty and blinked. Suddenly his head was growing longer, his muzzle was narrowing, and his golden fur was turning a dark gray. It only lasted a moment, and then he was Monty again.

Cassidy's breath caught in her throat and she felt her legs grow weak. She grabbed the edge of the closet to steady herself and then carefully stepped off the chair and crossed the room. She picked up Monty in her arms, and he snuggled his head against her. He was the same lovable cat. *So what did I see?*

His body and legs had been longer, his tail a thick gray brush — *like the animal I saw in the alley.*

Monty jumped out of her arms and ambled out of her room to the hallway. Cassidy stared after him. *Could my eyes have just been playing tricks on me?* she wondered. *After all,* she told herself, *I was thinking about the animal I saw when I was with Eliza.*

Cassidy tried to shake off the weird creepy feeling and opened the carved wooden box. She emptied the five gold coins onto her bed and picked up the one engraved with the image of some sort of animal. She turned it over and swallowed hard.

Three small lines on the back. *The third coin,* she thought, a sense of dread coursing through her body. The coin engraved with the winged snake had one small line on the back, and the coin with the waves and hollow eyes, representing the plague ghost, was marked with two lines. *And this one has three lines. I guess that means . . . the third demon?*

Turning the coin over, she ran her finger across the image of the animal on the front — the sharp nose and ears, the curled tail. *It kind of looks like a fox,* she thought. *And it definitely looks like the animal I saw in the alley. So what does this mean? That the fox demon is here?*

She'd learned that the image on each coin was connected to some strength or supernatural power of the demon. The strength of the first demon, the winged snake, was in its poison. The second demon, the plague ghost, had the ability to curse the city with floods and thunderstorms.

As Cassidy turned the heavy gold coin over in her hand, she pictured the animal she had seen in the alley. *So what kind of powers would a fox demon have?*

Cassidy remembered the way it had turned, pausing for a moment to look at them. *So what was so weird about that?* After all, the fox would have heard their voices. Naturally it would have noticed them. *But it was more than that,* Cassidy had to admit. *It was the way the fox looked at me—almost like it was seeing inside me.*

There was something else, too. It had seemed to *talk* to her—or at least to try to communicate in some way. And then she recalled hearing the words in her head as the fox nodded at her and then sneered—or maybe even smiled: *"Come with me."*

Chapter Six

The following Wednesday, Cassidy and the other Wing Chun students were astounded when their teacher, Master Lau, burst out of his office and crossed the gymnasium in no more than two or three leaps. He landed with perfect balance in the forward stance of tiger-style kung fu, his hands extended in the open-claw position of attack. Then he held the tiger's crouching stance, and Cassidy was sure he could leap from that position to just about anywhere else in the gym. It was all so sudden and powerful that it was almost as if Master Lau had *become* a tiger.

The students stood wide-eyed, amazed at

his speed and skill. Even Majesta, the cool and perfect cheerleader from Wilder High, looked absolutely awestruck. Only James Tang seemed utterly unimpressed with Master Lau's explosive demonstration.

The *shifu* stood erect now and waited for his students to bow, first to him and then to each other, before beginning class. "Students," he said, "the tiger is an aggressive and powerful animal. The tiger does not hesitate in any way, and its strike will maim or kill in a single blow."

As Cassidy listened, it occurred to her that she thought about these Wing Chun lessons in a totally different way now. *I may have to attack like a tiger someday,* she was thinking. *And if I do, I definitely want to know what I'm doing.*

Cassidy shuddered. She had first started taking martial arts classes to help her become more athletic and tone her body. *But now here I am actually using Wing Chun to fight demons!* When she battled the snake demon and then the plague ghost, she had used skills she had learned from Master Lau.

"The power of the tiger is generated in deep, rooted stances," Master Lau said as he demonstrated how the tiger can quickly spring forward from its crouch, taking its opponent by complete surprise. "The tiger has strong bones, ligaments, and tendons in its legs," he explained.

Cassidy was glad that she was a strong runner.

It would help her develop the strength necessary for this kind of drill. To attack like a tiger would require speed and power, but also efficiency of movement.

"And what do we know about the tiger's greatest weapon?" Master Lau asked his students. No one answered. Then, in another series of astonishing leaps, he landed in front of James Tang, his open hand positioned as a tiger's claw just inches from James's face. "This," he said, taking a swipe in front of James but not touching him, "*this* is the tiger's weapon. As you can imagine, few victims are lucky enough to survive a blow from the tiger's powerful claws."

What is Master Lau trying to do? Cassidy wondered. *Maybe he's trying to get some kind, any kind, of response from James.* She tried to read James's face, but it was impossible. He had barely acknowledged the *shifu's* aggressive move, making quick eye contact at first but then looking away. Since the day James first showed up, he had made no secret of the fact that he was only in the class because his father made him go.

Cassidy knew James didn't want to be there, but she was thankful for whatever—his dad, fate, destiny—had placed James Tang in her class. She had always enjoyed going to Wing Chun, but now she couldn't wait to get to class to see James.

From the first paired drill with James, Cassidy knew that his skills were beyond those of almost everyone in the class. But she had also noticed that he seemed to hold back if he suspected Master Lau was watching him. It was obvious that James wanted absolutely zero attention from Master Lau, so Cassidy knew that he must have hated the *shifu*'s tiger-stance demonstration, which brought them face-to-face.

As Master Lau walked back to the front of the class, Cassidy and James exchanged glances. *What was that?* mouthed James, who seemed irritated rather than impressed by Master Lau's performance. Cassidy shrugged, then went back to paying attention to Master Lau. *Maybe if James would just try to get to know Master Lau—even a little—he might like him.* But it had been almost five months since James started class. If he hadn't warmed up to Master Lau by now, it seemed unlikely that he ever would.

For the next thirty minutes, Master Lau led the students through the various stances of tiger-style Wing Chun. "Purpose is of key importance," Master Lau explained. "When springing forward to attack, do not hesitate, do not question. Once the tiger makes the decision to attack, his purpose is simple: to kill."

Before ending class, Master Lau held up his hand to make an announcement. "Three Wing Chun schools in Seattle have been honored with an invitation to participate in a tournament in Hong Kong this coming August," he explained. "I will be submitting the names of four students of mine who have the skills necessary to compete. During the next few classes I intend to look closely at your abilities and"—the *shifu*'s eyes rested on James—"your attitude."

After Master Lau dismissed them and returned to his office, the class buzzed with excitement. "Hong Kong! We're going to Hong Kong!" Cassidy's friend Luis exclaimed as they walked toward the locker rooms. "Can you believe it?"

"Wow, Luis, you're pretty sure of yourself," Cassidy teased. "Master Lau probably doesn't even know who he's choosing himself."

"Come on, you know I'm right," Luis said.

"Right about what?" Majesta asked, joining them at the water fountain. "Wait, let me guess. You two are already planning your trip to Hong Kong?"

"So what if we are?" Luis said. "We've learned a lot in this class, and we're pretty good."

"Sure," Majesta said. "But Master Lau said he can only pick four students. We have no idea what the competition might be in the other classes."

As James walked past the group, Majesta grabbed his arm to stop him. "I think there's one sure bet, though. Looks like you'll be getting a free trip back to Hong Kong, James."

James shrugged. "There are no sure bets—or free rides," he said. "Besides, even if Lau does choose me, I'm not sure I'd go."

Luis caught Cassidy's eye as James walked away. "Could he be any more full of himself?"

"He's not full of himself," Majesta said. "He's just really, really good."

"Sure, whatever, Majesta." Luis shook his head

and looked at Cassidy. "Meet you at the bus stop?"

"No bus for me tonight, Luis. My mom's picking me up," Cassidy told him. "I'll see you at school tomorrow." She headed into the locker room to change, wondering if James really would refuse to go if Master Lau chose him.

Outside, a few students stood in small groups waiting for rides or for the bus. Cassidy walked out of the gym and saw James at the bottom of the steps.

"You need a ride somewhere, James?" Cassidy asked, bounding down the stairs. She slowed down and then worried that her voice gave away how very much she *hoped* that he did need a ride. "My mom's on her way," she added casually.

"Nah, thanks anyway. My dad's coming."

Cassidy stuck her thumb into the strap of her backpack. "Um, I sort of took your advice," she said. "I set up a shrine in my room."

James looked at her. "Seriously?"

"Yeah." She told James about the antiques shop and the visit from her ancestors on the lake. "Just before she disappeared, my great-grandmother said something about demons waiting for me." She paused, wanting to get the wording exactly right. "In the *'shadowy darkness of the world—and of the mind.'*"

James frowned. "Whoa, she actually said, 'of

the mind'? Spooky."

"Yeah," Cassidy said. "Weird, huh? I have no idea what it means. Anyway, I put up this shrine and . . . I don't know. It's nice. I guess it makes me feel better. And like you said, it couldn't hurt."

James laughed, and Cassidy wondered if he was laughing at her. But then he said, "You're really something, Crane Girl." Cassidy wondered if James was flirting with her. He'd first called her Crane Girl when he saw her perfect crane stance in class.

"Your tiger stance looked good today," Cassidy said. "At least when Master Lau wasn't looking."

"Yeah? Well, yours looked good, too — as usual. Are you always so perfect?" James asked, and smiled at her. *That smile . . . his eyes . . .*

"I'm not perfect," she said, feeling a little thrill.

"Come on, Cassidy, your skills are, like . . . well, way beyond what any of us can do in there." His eyes narrowed as he studied her. "You've improved so much since I started in the fall. It's like you've shifted into a whole other gear. You know that, don't you?"

"I — I guess . . ." She'd sensed that her Wing Chun skills were improving. And with the possibility of demons coming after her, she was practicing every chance she got. But she was pretty sure there was more to it. Could the power of the coins be helping? Or maybe even her ancestors?

Almost as if James had read her mind, he said, "So has there been any demon action lately? The third coin—that's the one with the animal on it, right?"

"Right." Cassidy nodded, impressed that he remembered the details. *Is that because he's interested in the coins—or interested in me?* "Actually," she said quickly, before she got herself all distracted, "I'm starting to think it might be a fox." She told him about the animal she saw downtown with Eliza and then about the way Monty seemed to morph into a fox and then back.

"It didn't happen to be a gray fox, did it?" James asked. He was looking over her shoulder.

Cassidy gaped at him. "How did you know?"

"Well, don't turn around, okay? But there's a gray fox standing at the corner."

"James!" Cassidy gasped. She started to turn, but he put a hand on her shoulder to stop her.

"No, don't look," he warned in a low voice. "It's weird, it's, like, seriously checking us out."

Cassidy felt the hairs along the back of her neck rise. "That's what it did when I was with Eliza. It must be following me."

"Let's find out," James said. "When I count to three, let's go after it, see what it does."

"What?"

"One . . ."

"Chase it? James, are you—"

"Two . . ." James was slowly sliding the backpack off his shoulder.

"Three!" he said, and took off running.

❀ Chapter Seven

Cassidy dropped her backpack and turned in time to see the fox's tail disappear around the corner just as James hit the street in a full run. *What does he think he's doing? Is he crazy?*

She caught up to James halfway down the block, surprised to see him facing an angry older woman who was holding a small brown terrier in her arms. The little dog snarled and barked, snapping as if it wanted to jump out of the woman's arms and onto James's neck.

"Shame on you!" she shouted at James. "You scared us both half to death!"

"I'm sorry, really," James said. "I thought—"

Cassidy noticed that he couldn't finish the sentence. What would he say? *I thought your dog was a fox demon?*

The woman gave James a final, furious look and walked away, comforting the still-snarling dog.

James turned to look at Cassidy. "It was a fox — definitely a fox," he said, trying to catch his breath after the quick sprint. "Kind of medium-sized, gray fur, sharp ears. I chased it around the corner, then I saw this woman farther up the street walking her dog. Next thing I know, the fox sort of, I don't know, sort of *changed* into the dog. Like, entered its body or took it over or something."

Cassidy suppressed a shudder. "It's the third demon, isn't it?" She tried to keep her voice normal.

"Good chance." James's voice was as deliberately casual as hers. "It had these freaky yellowish claws. Definitely not a normal fox. And when we were talking before, it stood there at the corner watching us — like, *really* watching us."

Cassidy nodded, remembering the way it had looked at her and Eliza. "So how am I supposed to fight a fox demon?" she cried, her voice rising.

"You know the saying 'tricky like a fox'?"

"I thought it was 'crazy like a fox,'" Cassidy said, thinking that there had been nothing crazy about the fox she had seen earlier; it seemed to know exactly what it was doing.

"Yeah, I think it means the same thing, but in mythology the fox is usually a *trickster* sort of character—same with the raven."

Cassidy's eyes widened. "Like with Monty! I thought my eyes were playing tricks on me, but it was the fox."

"Exactly," James said. "That's the demon's strength, messing with your mind. I think maybe that's why the coin has a fox on it."

Cassidy threw up her hands in frustration. "Okay, but I still don't know what I'm supposed to do," she said. "Can a fox demon look like anything it wants? I mean, it changed into Monty *and* that dog."

"I'm not sure, Cass," James said. "I'll check my dad's books again and see if I can find anything." James's father, who taught Chinese literature and mythology at the university, had an extensive library in their house on Bainbridge Island.

"That would be great," Cassidy said. "Your dad's library is amazing." *Maybe James will ask me back to his house—to help with the research like before,* she thought.

But James said nothing as they walked back toward Master Lau's studio. When they reached the corner, Cassidy saw her mother pull up to the curb.

Cassidy grabbed her backpack and was heading to the car when a bird with the blackest feathers she'd ever seen flew down to the sidewalk and landed near her feet. The sudden movement startled her and she sucked her breath in quickly, her heart pounding. The bird, its black eyes shining, peered up at her. It opened its yellow beak wide and screeched twice before flying away in a dark frenzy of feathers.

"Tricky like a fox—or a *raven*?" she said, looking over at James. He was watching the bird fly over the gymnasium and out of sight.

"Be careful, Cass," James said, looking back at her with an intensity in his dark eyes that surprised her. *He looks worried, which means he cares about me—at least on some level,* Cassidy realized.

"Be really careful," he said again.

☙☙☙☙☙

At dinner that night, Cassidy told her parents about the tournament in Hong Kong. "That is so exciting, honey," her father said. "In fact, just the other day, I was thinking about planning a family trip to Hong Kong. I've been scanning those photos, and I realized how little I know about my own family."

Cassidy had a momentary vision of her ancestors, standing shoulder to shoulder on the lake that morning. "That would be great, Dad," she said. "I'd love to know more about my family. Both sides."

Wendy looked at Cassidy and smiled. "Me too. We get so caught up in the *present*. I think it would be great to take a look at our past—learn more about our families, what they were like. It might tell us more about who we are."

"Our destiny is a path," Cassidy said. "It's both where we've been and where we're going."

Cassidy noticed her mother and father exchange a look. "That's beautiful, sweetheart," Wendy said, and reached over and touched her hand. "Did you just make that up?"

"Uh, I don't think so," Cassidy replied, trying to remember where she'd heard those words. *My great-grandmother said them to me,* she remembered. "I . . . actually, I guess I just heard it somewhere."

ⓢⓢⓢⓢⓢ

Back in her room, Cassidy picked up the photograph of her grandfather that her dad had given her for the shrine. The picture showed a young man with a serious but kind face. He was smiling slightly and looked as if he had just said something before the photo was snapped. There was a shadow on the ground that stretched from the lower edge of the photo almost to her grandfather's feet, belonging to whoever took the photo. *Was it his wife?* Cassidy wondered. *My grandmother, the one who gave me my Chinese name—Mingmei?*

Cassidy touched her finger to the white streak in her grandfather's dark hair, trying to figure out how old he'd be now. *Maybe sixty, sixty-five?* She visualized the stranger who had given her the coins.

She shook her head. *It couldn't have been my grandfather. Dad said he died in a boating accident long before I was born.*

She returned the photograph to the shrine as Monty bounded into the room. When she sat at her computer, he leaped into Cassidy's lap. "Wanna check your e-mail, Monty?" she asked him, powering up her laptop. He looked up at her and crinkled his nose, rubbing his head against her. Then he reached out and slapped the space bar with purpose.

Cassidy laughed. "Whoa, there, cat, give it a minute." As she watched the screen come to life, she absentmindedly massaged Monty's small, warm paw, examining the soft pad and his tiny, razor-sharp claws. She remembered how Master Lau had pounced and landed in front of James, his hand extended like a tiger's massive and deadly paw. Cassidy pictured herself attacking like that—without hesitation.

Monty looked up at her and then smacked the keyboard again. Her in-box popped up on the screen. She clicked on an e-mail from James with the words "fox info" in the subject line.

C.

Found this in one of my dad's books: *"The fox demon is a trickster and a shape-shifter. His weapons are illusion and madness."* Remember what your ancestor said about a demon hiding in your mind? Maybe this is what she meant.

J.

That was it? Cassidy read the e-mail over again. *His weapons are illusion and madness.* What kind of Wing Chun skills could possibly work against some demon who played tricks and mind games?

She sent a brief reply to James: *Thanks for the info. But what am I supposed to do?*

Just as she hit Send, she heard a tapping at her window. Not a loud, insistent tapping, but a steady *tap . . . tap . . . tap.*

Cassidy fought back a rush of nerves and sat frozen in her chair as the constant rapping thrummed in her head like the ceaseless swings of a pendulum. It reminded her of the time the plague ghost first appeared to her at her bedroom window. *Please don't let this be what I think it is.*

Suddenly, against her will, Cassidy found herself standing up and gently placing Monty on the floor. *Tap . . . tap . . . tap.* She began moving slowly across the room toward the window—and realized that she was utterly helpless to stop herself. *Tap . . . tap . . . tap.* Something—the *something* that was out there—urged her forward with each persistent beat. *Tap . . . tap . . . tap . . . come . . . with . . . me.*

Chapter Eight

Cassidy saw her hands reach out to the window as if they weren't her own, as if there was nothing they could do but follow the pulsing command of the deliberate, unrelenting message. *Come with me. Come with me.* That's what the message sounded like. She watched, as if in a trance, as a bird's yellow beak struck the windowpane again and again in perfect, steady time.

She was certain it was the same bird that had flown down to her feet in front of Master Lau's. All she had to do was open the window and follow it, step off the ledge and into the chilly black night.

She paused, her hands resting lightly on the window. The raven's eyes met Cassidy's through the glass pane. The pale moonlight illuminated the bird's purple-black feathers as it continued tapping—the raps more insistent now, as if it were drumming a message into her brain. *Come with me.*

No! her mind seemed to scream, struggling to form even that one word. *"No!"* she cried again, this time aloud. And in that brief moment there was just the slightest pause in the tapping, just enough that the steady pulse was thrown off—enough to break the hypnotic spell of its rhythm.

It's the demon, she realized. *It's taken the form of a bird. James said it was a shape-shifter—that its weapons are illusion and madness.*

The creature stopped tapping and tilted its head. It looked at Cassidy with an intensity that made her shudder. *It's trying to get in my mind!*

Like an explosion of ginger-colored fur and claws, Monty suddenly leaped to the window ledge with such force that Cassidy heard the panes of glass rattle in the frame. A low guttural cry came from his throat, primitive, even junglelike.

The raven flew away in a fury of black feathers. It came back down again, just once, and rapped the window sharply with its yellow beak before screeching loudly and then soaring away into the night.

👁👁👁👁👁

During morning assembly, Cassidy told Eliza about the strange, dark bird. Eliza turned pale when she heard how it had tried to lure Cassidy to the window. "Was it trying to get you to jump or something?" Eliza asked in horror. "Do you think it was trying to *take* you?"

"I don't know," Cassidy admitted. "But I'm sure it's going to be back—as *something*."

"Terrific," Eliza said. "You don't even know what it's going to *be*, Cass—a bird, a fox." She threw up her hands. "This is too much, okay? This is crazy stuff—*evil* stuff—and you've got to make it stop."

"I wish I could make it stop, but I can't!" Cassidy said in desperation. "The only thing I can do is be prepared."

"Prepared?" Eliza echoed. "How exactly are you supposed to prepare to fight something like that weird bird thing? Obviously you *weren't* prepared," she went on in a heated tone. "It sounds like you were ready to follow it right out your window."

"That's not true," Cassidy protested. "I said the word *no*. I was resisting it—*with my mind*. And then Monty came running in and—"

"And probably saved your life!" Eliza cut in. "You better give that cat some extra kitty treats."

Cassidy smiled. "I already have." But she wondered: *What would have happened if Monty hadn't been there? Would I have been able to resist the bird? Eliza's right. How can I prepare to fight a demon that can get into my mind?*

As soon as school was out, Cassidy went to her favorite place to practice Wing Chun—a deserted playground in the middle of an abandoned, dilapidated housing complex. Broken wooden benches lined the edges of the small park where mothers once watched their children play on the swings and slides and monkey bars. An old sandbox was littered with trash that had blown through and gotten caught inside its frame.

Cassidy had read an article about kung fu training in out-of-the-way places and recognized immediately that the empty playground's ladders, monkey bars, and wide-open spaces would be an ideal spot to train when she couldn't go to Master Lau's. She really, really wanted to go to Hong Kong, and that meant extra practice. *Lots of extra practice.*

But Cassidy also realized there was a more immediate reason to increase the number of hours she practiced her Wing Chun skills. *I have to be ready,* she told herself. *Or at least as ready as I can be—since I don't even know for sure what I'll be fighting.*

She stood at the base of the slide, facing the metal ladder. She worked on her kicks, honing her accuracy and balance by kicking between the ladder's rungs at different heights. Next she went inside the metal cage of the monkey bars, punching in the spaces between the bars and blocking imaginary kicks. She let Master Lau's words form a continual loop in her head. *The central aim of kung fu is to develop one's physical and mental power. But the* ultimate *aim of kung fu is a total unity of mind, body, and spirit.*

Hands out, strike, retreat, turn, strike again, block, turn, kick!

"What did those monkey bars ever do to you?"

Cassidy whirled around to see Eliza just stepping into the playground.

"What are you doing here?" Cassidy asked. She ducked under the monkey bars and headed toward Eliza.

"I figured we could hang out," Eliza said. "Cheerleading practice got canceled. Coach Rogers has a virus or something."

"You followed me?" Cassidy said, feeling a little embarrassed at being watched during her drills. "You didn't have to do that. You could have just asked me where I was going."

"I wasn't following you in a *sneaky* kind of way," Eliza said. "I saw you turn the corner and I called you, but I guess you didn't hear me. Then I saw you sort of disappear into the trees. And when you started your drills, I didn't want to interrupt you."

Eliza scanned the playground. "It's kind of cool back here, Cass. Well, maybe just a little spooky," she added. "But kind of all *Secret Garden*—you know, like a secret *city* garden or something."

Cassidy stifled a surge of impatience. Her practice had been going so well—she had really started to hit a zone when Eliza interrupted. "So, what's up?" Cassidy asked.

"I don't know," she said. "It's just—" She shrugged. "I guess I'm really bummed about the move. I don't know why my mom's doing this. It's so . . . selfish!"

"Come on, Eliza, you know your mom," Cassidy said. "She won't go through with it." Mrs. Clifford had talked about moving a gazillion times and always changed her mind.

"She's talking about it, like, all the time now." Eliza kicked a dented soda can. "Maybe I'll just run away and come live here." She gestured toward the empty apartment houses. "All the gray gloom and doom fits my mood. And at least I'd still be in Seattle."

Cassidy gazed across the deserted playground at the long shadows cast by the vacant buildings. "You're not going to run away," Cassidy teased. "You like hot showers too much."

It was clear from the look Eliza gave Cassidy that she wasn't in the mood for joking. She sighed and stared down at the uneven ground.

Cassidy's mind wandered back to the practice. She had been feeling so strong, so powerful. Her warm-up kicks and punches had been right on target, and her mind had been leading her through every move—a seamless fusion of thought and action.

"Are you even listening to me?" Eliza asked.

"What—oh yeah, of course," Cassidy said,

flustered because she hadn't really been paying attention. She had been thinking that she still had another hour for drills before the sun went completely down. "Look, why don't I call you when I get home tonight? We can talk some more then."

Eliza crossed her arms over her chest. "Oh, I get it. You want to get back to your training. I'm, like, keeping you from practicing, right?"

"I'm sorry, Eliza," Cassidy said. "But yeah, I'm training more because I really want to go to this tournament in Hong Kong. I have to be good—"

"No," Eliza interrupted her. "It's not just about going to Hong Kong. You're—I don't know—preparing for a fight, aren't you? A real fight with some kind of freaky demon creature that probably wants to *kill* you!"

"No—I mean, yeah, maybe I am—but I have to. I have to be ready to—" Cassidy tried to explain, but again Eliza cut her off.

"You keep saying that, but you *don't* have to. Cassidy, you're a fourteen-year-old girl, not some superhero ninja in a martial-arts movie." She waved her hands impatiently, her voice rising in pitch and in volume. "This is real life! *Your* life! You should be doing normal things—going shopping, having sleepovers, arguing with your parents—not preparing for some kind of *battle*!"

"Do you think I want this stuff to be happening to me?" Cassidy demanded.

"You're really into all this training," Eliza countered.

Cassidy wasn't sure what to say. There was a lot to this destiny thing that she didn't really understand, but somehow she knew she had to be ready to fight.

"I don't know what to tell you," Cassidy said at last. "All I know is that so far I've had to fight two really powerful demons. And I'm pretty sure there are three more waiting for me. I have to be ready. And that means that I have to practice because I have to be really, really good. Don't you understand that?"

"Well, don't you understand that maybe I'm worried about you?" Eliza snapped. "And maybe *that's* why I followed you here?" She spun around and headed toward the dark line of trees to the path that would lead her back to Bay Street.

Cassidy watched Eliza walk away, wondering if she should stop her, but then decided against it. It was probably better to let her have some time to cool off. *I'll call her tonight. I'll try to make her understand.* But Cassidy wondered if that was possible. *I don't even understand it myself, so what am I supposed to say to Eliza?*

Chapter Nine

By the time Cassidy started for home, the sun was low in the sky and there was a briskness in the air that made her pull her corduroy jacket close to her body for warmth. Just before reaching the opening in the trees, she heard the crackle of dried leaves. She turned back around and saw a little girl walking toward one of the swings. The girl sat down on the wooden seat and began swinging back and forth, the rusty chains creaking above her.

Cassidy scanned the area to see if the girl was with a parent, but there didn't seem to be anybody else around. *Somebody must know she's here,* Cassidy thought.

She's too young to be out here by herself.

Cassidy walked over to the little figure on the swing, whose legs dangled above the ground. Her long dark hair was mussed and hung loose down her back. *How old is she?* Cassidy wondered. *Four or five, maybe? Why is she out here alone?*

Cassidy approached her slowly, careful not to scare her. "Hi," she said. "Are you okay? Do you need some help?"

The little girl stopped swinging and looked up, her large gray eyes wide and shiny with tears. "I'm okay," she said. "I just wanna play."

"Do you live close by?" Cassidy asked, hoping the little girl was old enough to know her address.

"In there," the little girl said, twisting and pointing to the apartment buildings behind her. "But I don't know which one. My mommy is in there, but I can't find her."

The girl swiveled back around and began swinging again, back and forth, the chains creaking steadily. *Creak . . . creak . . . creak.*

She lives in the abandoned apartments? Cassidy's forehead wrinkled as she frowned. *But there's no heat or electricity—how could somebody live there?* She looked again at the little girl and noticed the way she was dressed—thin gray sweater and pants that were too short and left her tiny ankles looking exposed and cold. Cassidy realized that living in an abandoned building was probably better than living on the street.

"Maybe I can help you find her," Cassidy said. *Then I'll call Mom and we'll get you both in a warm shelter somewhere,* she added silently.

"She's lost," the little girl said. "I just wanna swing now. You can play, too. Swing with me."

How am I going to get her off those swings? Cassidy wondered. *I can't just leave her out here.*

The playground was silent except for the steady creak of the rusted chains as the little girl swung back and forth, back and forth.

"Swing with me," the little girl said. "And then I'll go find Mommy."

Cassidy sat down on the swing next to the little girl, hoping to gain her confidence so that she could help her.

The only sounds were the rhythmic creaks of the rusty iron chains that seemed now to reverberate against the walls of the buildings. *Creak . . . creak . . . creak.* The little girl matched her swing to Cassidy's. For several minutes, neither Cassidy nor the little girl spoke. Cassidy could see why the little girl wanted to swing—the rhythm and even the creaking sounds were soothing.

At last the little girl stopped swinging and jumped down to the ground. "We can go now," the little girl said. "My mommy's in that building."

Cassidy slowed her swing to a stop and stood. She turned to face the three large rectangular buildings looming behind them, each probably six stories high.

Although it was nearly dark, Cassidy could see broken windows and peeling paint.

"She's up there," the girl said, and pointed to the top floor of the middle building. "Will you come with me?" she asked, and held out a small hand in a worn brown glove.

Cassidy started to reach out to take the girl's hand when she froze. The swings. They were still moving on their rusty chains. *Creak . . . creak . . . creak.*

"Come with me?" the little girl pleaded. She moved closer to Cassidy. *Creak . . . creak . . . creak.*

Something was wrong. Cassidy's mind raced as she tried to figure out what it was. *What's wrong with this picture? She's just a little girl and she needs help. So what . . . is . . . wrong?*

Creak . . . creak . . . creak.

Cassidy looked at the girl's hand. Two of the fingers of the old glove were almost worn through. Two tiny fingernails were visible through the tattered fabric of the glove.

Cassidy felt a chill run down her spine as she remembered the words that had formed in her head when the dark bird tapped at her window. *Come . . . with . . . me.*

She looked down at the little girl, whose dark hair was almost purple black. The hand she held up to Cassidy was small, and the two exposed fingernails were a sickly yellowish color, exactly the color of the bird's beak . . . *and the fox's claws.*

Chapter Ten

"No!" Cassidy cried, and yanked her hand away.

The little girl let out an inhuman noise—something between a laugh and a howl—that made Cassidy's blood run cold. The girl ran, changing with each step so that by the time she was halfway to the opening between the trees, she was down on all fours and covered in fur.

Cassidy felt frozen in place. Her heart pounded against her chest. She wanted to look away from the hideous transformation, but she couldn't. A weak security light near the edge of the playground illuminated the fox so that Cassidy could see it, fully formed now. Its long muzzle and sharp ears were in perfect silhouette against the trees.

She watched in astonishment as the creature leaped, not through the opening, but *straight up above the trees!* Cassidy's breath caught tight in her throat as the fox changed again. Dark wings formed and spread wide, and its nose changed into a sharp yellow beak. The raven flew over the tops of the fir trees, issuing a long, piercing screech before disappearing into the early evening dusk.

Now that the *thing* was out of sight, Cassidy felt her legs weaken. She dropped to the cold ground, her knees striking the hard, uneven pavement. After a few shaky breaths, she reached out to the metal leg of the swing set and pulled herself to her feet. *What would have happened if I'd followed the girl—the demon—into the apartment?* She forced the thought out of her mind and hurried out of there.

As Cassidy walked home, even the most ordinary things seemed menacing. She felt as if she were holding her breath, expecting the creature to appear around the next corner. It could be anything— *A dog darting down an alley, a bird at the window, a lost child on a playground . . .*

Just before reaching her house, Cassidy had another confusing thought. *Why didn't the fox demon attack? There was no one else around on that playground. Why did it run when I figured out what it was?*

She puzzled over the answer, thinking back to

the little girl's strange laugh and then her howl. *It's a game,* Cassidy realized, coming to a complete stop at her front door. *A very sick game. The fox demon is playing with me—illusion and madness are its weapons.*

ᗡᗡᗡᗡᗡ

The next morning, the phone woke Cassidy. "Hello?" she answered groggily, wondering why her parents hadn't picked up. "Cassidy, is Eliza with you?" There was worry, almost panic, in Sarah Clifford's voice.

Cassidy rubbed the sleep from her eyes. The middle school was closed for its annual maintenance day, and Cassidy had planned to sleep a little later and then go for a morning run. "No, Eliza's not here—I mean, unless she's downstairs or something."

"Would you go check, please?"

The house was empty. It was a bit later than Cassidy had realized, and both Simon and Wendy had already left for work. There was a note on the table from Cassidy's mom, telling her to have a good day and to clean Monty's litter box.

Cassidy picked up the telephone extension in the kitchen. "Ms. Clifford, I'm downstairs, and Eliza's not here either."

"We had an argument last night," Sarah Clifford told Cassidy. "It looks like she slept in her bed, but she's not here this morning. I know that school is closed today, so I thought that maybe she came over to see you."

Poor Eliza, Cassidy thought. *She follows me because she's worried about me and wants to talk, but we get into an argument. Then she goes home and fights with her mother about this crazy move. She must have been seriously bummed.* Cassidy pressed her lips together, an idea forming. *What did Eliza say—that she should run away to the abandoned apartments?*

"I think I might know where she is," Cassidy told Eliza's mom. "Let me go check, and then I'll call you back."

"Thanks, Cassidy. I know that Eliza's upset about moving, but she didn't have to run away. She could have *talked* to me about it."

Eliza has been trying to talk to you for months now, Cassidy thought. "Well, I'm sure she's fine—just upset, you know?"

"I'll call Tamika, too," Sarah Clifford added. "And some of her other cheerleader friends."

"That's a good idea," Cassidy said. But she felt certain that she would find Eliza at the playground—the playground that Eliza liked because the "gloom and doom" matched her mood.

❧❧❧❧❧

When Cassidy stepped through the opening in the trees, she was struck again by just how quiet it seemed inside the enclosure of tall buildings and trees—as if all the usual city traffic sounds were absorbed by the heavy concrete and foliage. Her eyes swept across the playground, and she spotted Eliza sitting cross-legged at the top of the slide. Eliza wore a heavy sweatshirt, and she had the hood pulled close around her face with her hands tucked under her arms.

Cassidy hoped that she could find the right thing to say to her friend. "Hey, Eliza!" she called out as she jogged across the playground.

Eliza's head jerked toward Cassidy. She looked surprised—and, Cassidy noticed, *really afraid.* "No, Cass, don't come any closer!"

"Come on down, Clifford, let's talk," Cassidy said. "Your mom called me. She's worried."

But Eliza just shook her head and pointed. That's when Cassidy saw it—the gray fox stepping out of the morning shadows cast by the dark buildings. The animal trotted to the bottom of the slide and looked up at Eliza and then back at Cassidy. Its dark muzzle opened slightly, revealing sharp, yellowed teeth. It began pacing, walking a circle around the slide but fixing its gleaming eyes on Cassidy.

"Eliza, listen to me," Cassidy said, trying to keep her voice steady. "I'm going to lure the fox away, okay? He'll follow me. Once he's far enough away, you slide down and run. It's me he wants. He won't chase you."

"I can't," Eliza said. "It's—"

"Yes, you can!" Cassidy insisted, realizing that Eliza must be paralyzed with fear. "Don't be afraid—just slide down or climb down the ladder. I swear, I'm the one he's after."

"No, I mean, I *can't*," Eliza said again. "The slide's not . . . it's not *real*!" She reached out her hand and Cassidy watched in disbelief as Eliza passed her hand right *through* the slide.

It's an illusion, Cassidy realized with horror. *The slide that Eliza is sitting on is just an illusion! She has no way to get down!*

❀ *Chapter Eleven*

It's not possible! Cassidy's mind raced. *That slide was real yesterday. I used it in practice!*

The fox snarled, grabbing Cassidy's attention. It lifted its chin and bared its teeth, showing Cassidy sharp incisors, designed for ripping flesh from bones.

Focus! she ordered herself. *Worry about the slide later. Right now keep your eyes on that fox.*

The fox took a step toward Cassidy and then stopped and tilted its head. Wing Chun training had taught Cassidy to be aware of her opponent at all times. She noted the fox's posture and how it looked at her. She had no doubt that the fox was about to attack.

How do I fight a fox? she wondered. But before she could form a plan, the fox began to change. She watched in shock as its body elongated and its legs lengthened and became more muscular. The fox's head lost its long, sharp muzzle and grew larger as its mouth spread wide and formed powerful jaws. The creature lost its sleek gray coat and stripes began to form, deep orange against black in a jagged pattern the length of its body.

Cassidy couldn't believe what she was seeing. A raw fear gripped her heart. A full-grown tiger stood where the fox had been, its golden eyes fixed on her. The tiger's body was thick with muscle, and Cassidy knew that with one leap, the animal would be on top of her, ripping her apart. Master Lau's words came back to her: *A tiger's strike will maim or kill in a single blow.*

Eliza shrieked in terror from the top of the slide. Cassidy debated risking a glance at her, but she didn't dare take her eyes from the tiger's burning gaze. *I have to be ready.* But even as she thought the words, she realized how ridiculous they were. *There's no way to be ready for the attack of a tiger—I can't fight a—*

An image of Master Lau bounding across the studio floor—*becoming* a tiger as he went on the offensive—flashed across Cassidy's mind. She heard the *shifu's* words in her head—*The tiger does not hesitate in any way*—and before another thought crossed her mind, she acted. Immediately and forcefully, Cassidy covered the distance between herself and the large animal in one powerful leap, landing in the aggressive stance of tiger-style kung fu. Instinctively she reached for the closest weapon—a rusted pipe that lay on the edge of the cement playground.

The tiger, startled by Cassidy's sudden move, edged away. Cassidy knew she had to take advantage of the opportunity to strike before the tiger did.

Facing the beast, she raised the rusted pipe and struck fast, bringing it down on the tiger's neck. The tiger shook itself irritably and padded toward her.

Did it even feel that? she worried, backing away from the big cat. She came to an abrupt stop as her back hit the wall of a building. She could feel the tiger's hot breath on her face.

The tiger made a low, guttural sound, and its claws lashed out. Cassidy ducked to the side and struck hard with the pipe. The big cat snarled and staggered. She watched, disbelieving, as the tiger's image shimmered and wavered. In moments it was replaced with the huge, round, soft body of a spider. A tiger-sized spider!

Eliza shrieked above her, and Cassidy screamed and stumbled to get away from the terrifying creature. Then she stopped, knowing she had to face it.

She stared in horror at the unnatural creature that stood before her, trying to make sense of what she was seeing. Its dark, hairy legs quivered and twitched. The body of the spider was grayish, with darker stripes that radiated out from its center. Cassidy felt her stomach lurch. *So repulsive!*

The spider's eyes glittered and focused on her. It opened its mouth—a dark hole that contained two sharp sets of reddish fangs. The spider hissed, and the sound made Cassidy's blood turn to ice as eight enormous spindly legs moved toward her.

How am I supposed to fight this thing? Cassidy wondered frantically. But she had no time to think. The spider lunged toward her. In a fury of strikes and blocks, Cassidy dodged the spider's legs, swinging the pipe at whatever limb was closest.

This is like fighting four people at once! She felt herself tiring. *Its weakness, what is the spider's weakness?* She had to think fast as she moved and struck. *Its weakness is its body, or lack of one,* Cassidy realized with a sickening sense of horror. She would have to attack the spider's soft, disgusting body.

She fought her way through the cage of its eight legs and struck the spider's abdomen with the pipe. It shrieked, and Cassidy could actually feel it waver. As it began to fall, Cassidy backed away. She needed to catch her breath. Her lungs were raw, and her heart felt as if it were ready to burst out of her chest.

As the spider fell, it shimmered the way a mirage in a desert might, and then it began to fade. In its place, a dark robed figure lay in a heap.

Cassidy's breath quickened, the cold air searing her throat. She knew this battle wasn't over yet.

The creature slowly rose to its feet and stood

facing Cassidy. All Cassidy could see within the shadowed hood of the gray robe were two angry, glittering eyes—black with rage.

The thing lifted its arms, and the sleeves of the robe fell away from two large, furred hands that ended in sharp yellow claws. It pushed the hood away from its face, revealing long, iron gray hair. Cassidy shuddered as she saw the pointed ears and the mottled gray muzzle of a fox on the body of a man. The demon's upper lip curled over its teeth in a snarl.

The fox demon—this is its true image, she realized. *The tiger and the spider were both illusions. And now it's angry because I can see it for what it is.*

Cassidy's throat closed in fear as the creature slowly and deliberately ran the point of his blood-red tongue over an incisor. Baring his teeth in a low growl, the demon moved toward her.

"Do you like what you see?" the demon asked.

Cassidy stood paralyzed by terror as he let out a bloodcurdling howl that ended in a ragged laugh.

"I hope you've enjoyed my games," the fox demon said, his eyes glittering, cruel and savage. "Because they've only just begun."

Chapter Twelve

"Cassidy, *no*!" Eliza screamed.

Instinctively Cassidy turned at the sound of her name, and in that split second the fox demon struck. His claws slashed the air, aiming for Cassidy's face. She ducked the vicious blow at the last possible second.

Cassidy retreated two steps and then turned, bringing around a powerful kick that landed in the perfect center of the fox demon's chest. She heard the air whoosh from him as he reeled backward, staggering.

Strike now! Cassidy ordered herself. She remembered Master Lau's words again: *The tiger does not hesitate in any way.* She bounded forward, swinging the pipe—but the demon was ready for her and easily knocked it from her hand.

"That's better." The fox demon sneered. "Now let's see what kind of warrior you are."

Cassidy raised her right arm to deflect a blow that would have taken her down. Then she attacked with a flurry of strikes to the demon's chest and face.

With an incredible leap, the fox demon catapulted backward and onto the crossbar of the seesaw. He crouched there, golden eyes following her.

Cassidy lunged forward. The fox demon turned quickly and executed a sweeping kick, but she had anticipated this move and leaned backward just in time. She felt the rush of wind from his powerful kick and was thankful it hadn't made contact.

The fox demon spun dizzily from the force of his attempted move, but he gained control and came back around to face Cassidy. She was ready for him, bringing her striking arm down with a powerful blow to the back of his neck. He howled in pain and fell forward to his knees. *Now! Strike now—the final blow!* But before she could land a killing strike, he rolled away from her. He crouched at the bottom of the slide, panting hard—a white foam forming at his mouth.

Cassidy studied him, waiting for his next move. *He's getting weaker,* she realized. *But it's not over. He won't give up this easily.* She glanced at Eliza, still trapped at the top of the slide, white with fear. Almost as if in slow motion, the fox demon's eyes followed Cassidy's gaze to Eliza. Then he leaped to the top of the slide and yanked Eliza to her feet.

"No!" Cassidy shouted. "Leave her alone!"

"I think your friend would like to play, too!" the fox demon called down to Cassidy.

Eliza shrieked and pulled against her captor's grip. She beat at him with her other hand while kicking as hard as she could, but the creature held fast.

"Your fight is with me—not her!" Cassidy tried to step onto the bottom of the slide, but her foot passed right through it as if nothing was there. She ran around to the ladder and attempted to grab a rung, but again, there was no substance to it. Above her, the fox demon let out howls of shrill laughter that ripped the air like fingernails on a chalkboard.

This is crazy! I KNOW this is a slide! But the illusion created by the fox was too powerful. Cassidy couldn't find a way to climb it.

"Are you having fun?" the fox demon called down to Cassidy. "Because *we're* having lots of fun up here." He gripped Eliza's hands so that she couldn't hit him. Still she struggled to wrench herself free, twisting, kicking, and screaming.

Cassidy felt nausea rise at the back of her throat. She knew Eliza was fighting for her life.

I have to get up there! She scanned the dilapidated playground equipment that surrounded them, desperate to find something that could help her—and help Eliza. Her eyes rested on the swing set. *Is it possible?* She calculated the distance between the swing and the slide. *Yeah, I can do it—I HAVE to do it!*

She raced to the swing and pushed off with her legs. She propelled herself higher and higher—willing herself to swing in an ever-increasing arc that took her closer to the top of the slide.

One . . . two . . . THREE! Cassidy launched herself from the swing at the very peak of the arc, and for a moment it felt as if she were flying. The demon released Eliza as Cassidy landed on top of the slide. His claws slashed out, ripping through Cassidy's sweatshirt and slicing into her right arm.

Ignoring the pain, Cassidy grabbed the fox demon and pulled as hard as she could, knocking them off balance. They fell together—the fox demon hitting the frozen ground with a sickening thud.

Cassidy's fall was softer, and she rolled several times before rising to her feet, ready for whatever was to come. She circled the demon, watchful, ready, as he lay on a pile of broken concrete.

The fox demon began to shift again. *He can't be changing into yet another animal, can he?* Cassidy thought as she watched him closely. His shape grew smaller, and then the evil creature finally began to disintegrate. There was a whimpering sigh as the demon vanished.

The awful beast was gone once and for all, leaving nothing behind except a small pile of gray matted fur and several yellowed claws.

❧ Chapter Thirteen

"Eliza, it's safe," Cassidy said. She took a deep, shuddering breath. "You can come down now."

"How?" Eliza cried. "How am I supposed to get off this thing?"

"It really is a slide, Eliza," Cassidy explained. "That's what the fox demon did. He made you *believe* that it was just an illusion. But now that he's gone—" Cassidy climbed up to her friend. At the top of the slide she wrapped her arms around Eliza and finished her sentence. "Now we're safe."

After a quick, intense hug, Cassidy climbed down the ladder and Eliza slid down the front. Moments later they were both back on solid ground.

Eliza looked shaky, but the color was returning to her face. "God, Cass," she said. "I can't believe what just happened. You could have been—"

"I know," Cassidy said. "Are you okay? You were really fighting him up there." Then she grinned at her friend. "For someone who's never taken a kung fu class, you did okay."

"Cheerleading muscles," Eliza said, attempting to return the smile. "Yeah, I'm okay, except for—" She held out the palm of her right hand. "It's just a scratch from when I tried to pull away from him."

The scratch was angry and red but thankfully not deep. It extended in a straight line from Eliza's little finger diagonally across her palm to the fleshy pad of her thumb.

"He got you, too," Eliza said, and pointed to the rip in Cassidy's sleeve. Cassidy pulled back the flap of fabric and saw three faint pink lines where her arm had made contact with the fox demon's sharp claws.

Eliza looked confused. "I saw him swipe you, Cass. But . . . almost nothing's there!"

Cassidy touched the already-healed lines on her arm where deep, bloody gashes should have been. "I heal really fast," she told Eliza. "It started happening after I killed the snake demon."

Eliza looked at Cassidy. "So that time you were making lunch for us and it looked like you cut your thumb, but then there was no mark, that was because it healed right away?"

"Yeah," Cassidy admitted. "That was the first time I noticed it. And there's other stuff, too—like, when I fell from the top of the slide just now I didn't get hurt."

Eliza nodded, trying to make sense of it. "This is seriously dangerous stuff that's going on. I'm worried about you, Cass. You have to stop doing this, fighting these things."

"You were here, Eliza. What am I supposed to do when demons show up? Say, 'I'd rather not fight, thank you,' and turn my back on them?"

Eliza grabbed Cassidy in a fierce hug. "I just *wish* so much that this wasn't happening!" she said.

Over her best friend's shoulder, Cassidy watched a slight breeze ruffle the pile of gray fur left behind by the fox demon. If only a wish *could* make the demons go away.

"Let's get out of here," Cassidy said, releasing Eliza. "We can talk about all this later."

"Definitely," Eliza agreed. "I feel like I could sleep for a hundred years."

"Some way to spend a free day, huh?"

"I never thought I'd hear myself saying this," Eliza said, "but I'd rather be in Mr. Poteet's literature class."

They walked through the opening between the trees, and Cassidy felt as if they were entering the normal world again. Eliza stopped for a moment and looked back toward the playground. "That really happened, didn't it?" she asked, confusion and bewilderment all over her face. "You just fought and killed that—whatever that thing was back there."

"Yeah, I did," Cassidy answered, realizing how hard it was for Eliza to believe what she had seen. *Maybe that's one reason it's easy to talk to James about it. James grew up with stories from Chinese mythology. So at least none of this is completely new to him.*

They walked the last block to Eliza's apartment house in silence. As Eliza took out her keys, Cassidy took another look at the scratch on her friend's hand. "You might want to put some ointment or something on that."

Eliza turned over her palm and looked at the red gash as if she were seeing it for the first time. She traced the line with her finger and then laughed.

"What's so funny?" Cassidy asked.

But Eliza only laughed harder and shook her head. She walked away from Cassidy and headed toward the apartment. Cassidy remained on the sidewalk, watching Eliza climb the steps to the front door. Eliza continued laughing, a high-pitched, shrieking laugh that echoed in Cassidy's head as she started down the sidewalk for home.

Chapter Fourteen

When Cassidy reached her house, she found that the gate that led to the backyard was slightly open. *Strange, I'm sure that wasn't open when I left.* She stepped into the backyard and saw immediately that one of the windowpanes in the back door had been broken out—the door was ajar and small shards of glass were scattered over the porch.

Cassidy's heart pounded and her mouth felt dry. *Somebody broke in! Somebody may still be in there!* She backed up, moving slowly and silently until she reached the front yard, where she whipped her cell phone from her pocket. She immediately dialed 911 and then her mom at the Happy Bunny Preschool.

The police arrived within minutes, and Cassidy's parents followed moments later. The Chens waited outside as the officers entered the house to scope out the crime scene.

It seemed forever before two officers came back outside.

"Well, nobody's in there," said a policeman who introduced himself as Officer Trenton.

"Weird time of day to break in, though," his partner said. "My guess is that somebody's been watching the house."

"Watching the house?" Cassidy's father asked. "You mean, waiting for us to leave for work and school?"

Cassidy's mom shook her head. "But Cassidy would have been here. School's out today, and she was going to sleep in."

"What time did you leave the house this morning?" Officer Trenton asked Cassidy.

"Around nine, I guess," she answered. "I went to meet my friend."

"Yeah, then I'd say whoever did this had been watching the house—waiting for you to leave."

"Officer," Wendy said, her voice tight with worry, "do you think whoever did it will be back?"

"Hard to say," he replied. "It's kind of a strange break-in, taking place in broad daylight like this. Also, whoever broke in left a real mess, like they were searching for something specific. I figure they were trying to find hidden money or jewelry, looking for something easy to pawn. They didn't touch any of the big items. The TV, stereo—all that stuff is still there."

"You'll need to go through and make a list of what's missing," the other officer continued while Trenton took a call that came in on his radio. "But don't get your hopes up over getting anything back. Stuff's probably out of state by now. Just a hit-and-run."

"Actually, that would make me feel better," Simon said. "I'd prefer a 'hit-and-run' to someone hanging around, still watching the house."

The officer handed Simon his card. "Call me if you see or hear anything else."

"So, you're saying it's safe to go inside now?" Wendy asked.

"Sure, ma'am, nobody's in the house. We checked everywhere. There is a scared little cat in your laundry room, though."

"Monty!" Cassidy cried, and ran for the door.

❧❧❧❧❧

Cassidy held Monty in her arms as she and her parents inspected the house. "It feels so creepy in here," Cassidy said, "knowing that some *thief* was walking around and touching our stuff."

"Yeah, it does feel very strange," her mother

agreed. She peered into the open drawer of an oak buffet in the dining room. "It's such a violation of personal space—oh no! They took my grandmother's silver!"

"Add it to the list, honey," Simon said, coming from the family room. "They were probably looking for small things they could carry out easily, maybe in a duffel bag. I'm just relieved they didn't touch the computer in my office."

"I wonder if they got my laptop," Cassidy said. "I'll go up and check out my room."

"You want us to go with you, sweetheart?" her mom asked.

"Nah, I'm okay," Cassidy said, heading up the steps, still holding Monty. *Weird,* she thought. *While I was fighting the fox demon, someone was breaking into our house. What would have happened if Ms. Clifford hadn't called me to say Eliza was missing? Would I have still been here? Would I have found myself fighting burglars instead of a fox demon?*

Cassidy stood in her doorway and surveyed the chaos. *Just great.* Her laptop was missing, and her papers and books were scattered all over the floor. She stepped into the room, taking care not to trip on anything. The small jewelry box that she kept on top of her dresser was open. All of her jewelry had been spilled out—but a quick glance told her nothing was missing. Her closet doors were also open, and boxes and shoes had been yanked out.

Cassidy sighed. "What a mess," she murmured into Monty's soft fur. He meowed as if in agreement.

What's that weird smell? she wondered, noticing an odd, sickly sweet odor in her room—*Maybe some kind of herb?* No, it was too sweet for that. The strange thing was that even though she couldn't identify the smell, it seemed familiar to her—*Maybe peaches—like, really rotting peaches?*

She noticed the top part of the carved wooden box that she had been given on her birthday poking out from under a sweater that had been tossed on the floor—the box that had contained the five gold coins. *Oh no!* Cassidy was certain that they would be gone. The owner of the Chinese Tiger had told her that the coins were made of solid gold.

Still holding Monty, she pushed aside a piece of rumpled tissue paper with the toe of her shoe. Her breath caught in surprise. There they were—all five coins scattered about on her rug—but still there! She knelt down to pick them up, and Monty jumped from her arms and ran back through her door to the hall.

She picked up the heavy coins one by one. When she picked up the one that was engraved with the image of the fox, it warmed against her palm. She looked closely at the image of the animal with the sharp ears and nose and then squeezed her hand again, the gold emitting a yellowish glow that grew warmer the harder she squeezed.

As she returned the coins to the wooden box,

she gazed around her room, noticing that her antique shrine had been overturned. *Awesome! They didn't take the shrine! They probably didn't know how much it's really worth.* She set the shrine upright again and then found her great-grandmother's hair comb and the jade dog charm on the floor near her bed and replaced them as well.

Cassidy was starting to feel better. Aside from the laptop, most of her things seemed to be here.

And then she realized that something else *was* missing.

Her grandfather's photograph.

She knelt down on the floor and searched under her bed, but nothing was there. *This is strange,* she thought, sinking back on her heels. *It's gotta be here somewhere.* She checked under everything that had been pulled out of her closet, but the photo was nowhere to be found.

This doesn't make sense, she told herself. *Why would a burglar take an old photograph—a photograph that wasn't even in a frame—but leave coins made of solid gold?*

🌸 Chapter Fifteen

"Need any help in here?" Wendy asked. She stood in Cassidy's doorway, gazing at the mess.

"I just need to put all this stuff back in my closet," Cassidy told her. "The only thing that's missing, though, is my laptop. Oh yeah, and that picture Dad gave me of his father. I can't find it anywhere."

"The photo?" Wendy asked, coming into the room and picking up scattered sweaters and pieces of board games. "It's probably here under some of this stuff. I can't imagine a burglar would want a picture of your grandfather."

"I've looked, Mom. It's weird, too, because the

coins weren't taken. They were dropped on the floor, but they're all there."

"The burglar must have been after something quick and easy to sell—like a laptop, the silver, that kind of thing. Old coins might be a little harder to get rid of."

"I guess," Cassidy said. "But it still doesn't explain why the picture's missing."

Wendy began refolding a pile of clothes on the floor. "I think this might be a good time to think about cleaning out your closet, Cass. You don't wear half of this stuff anymore." She held up a pair of jeans worn thin at the knees and ragged at the hem.

"I love those jeans," Cassidy said, taking them from her mother and holding them up at her waist. "But actually, you're right. I don't wear them because they're too short. Also, I've lost weight. They just don't fit right anymore."

"They're too short?" Wendy echoed. "Have you really gotten that much taller?"

"Yes," Cassidy said. "And now I'm stuck with these." She pulled on the pockets of the jeans she was wearing. "They're so totally uncool."

"So what are you trying to tell me?" her mother asked, smiling.

"Just that I could use a new pair of jeans," Cassidy said supersweetly.

"Well, why didn't you say so in the first place?" Wendy said with a wink. "We'll take a look this weekend. I think you could use a new sweatshirt, too." She pointed to the rip in Cassidy's sleeve.

"Uh, no, I actually kind of like my sweatshirt like this," Cassidy said, fingering the flap of loose cloth. "But they have some really cool jeans at VibeBuy. I tried on a pair this week that fit me perfectly."

Wendy's smile turned into a scowl. "Oh, Cass . . . you know VibeBuy is pretty pricey," her mother said. "You're still growing. I don't want to spend two hundred dollars on a pair of jeans that you'll outgrow in six months."

"I think you're forgetting that you still owe me for helping out at the Happy Bunny," Cassidy told her. "I worked after school three days last week."

Wendy laughed. "Your pay for three afternoons of work won't even pay for one leg of those jeans at VibeBuy."

"Come on, Mom," Cassidy said. "I always help out anytime you ask me."

"Yes, and I appreciate that very much," Wendy said. "Find something more reasonable and we'll talk."

It was clear to Cassidy that her mother wasn't budging on the jeans issue. So she made the executive decision to redirect her energies and call James and give him the lowdown on the day's events.

When her mom left, she closed her door and dialed the phone. "Hey, James, it's Cassidy," she said, nervously twirling her hair.

"Hey, what's up? Have a nice day off?"

"Well," Cassidy began, "I guess you could say it hasn't been boring . . ."

Cassidy told James about fighting the fox demon at the playground and then coming home to find that her house had been broken into. *He really listens to me,* she realized. *And he doesn't think all of this is just crazy—even though it kind of is.* She even considered telling James about Eliza's strange behavior, but she decided against it. Eliza might feel betrayed if she knew that Cassidy was discussing her with James.

"So, Cass," James said. "Are you thinking the break-in had anything to do with the coins?"

The question surprised her. She hadn't thought that at all. "What do you mean?" Cassidy asked. "They didn't even take the coins."

"I know," James said. "But it's kind of weird that the burglar came when you were out fighting one of the demons. You think somebody knew that's what you'd be doing?"

Cassidy considered the idea. "I don't think so," she said. "The officer said that somebody had probably been watching the house, waiting for me to leave. It was probably just a coincidence."

"Yeah, maybe," James said, not sounding convinced. "Any ideas on why they left the coins?"

"My mom thinks it's because the coins would be hard to sell."

Less than five minutes after they hung up,

James called back. Cassidy was beyond thrilled to hear his voice.

"I just found this," he said. "Listen up, okay? 'Certain charms, amulets, and objects of magic are imbued with the power of possession, meaning that the object may only be given, never taken.'"

"And you're telling me this because—"

"The coins, Cass. You know they're heavy-duty magic. Well, maybe they're imbued with the power of possession."

Cassidy was silent, trying to make sense of this new information.

"I think whoever broke into your house wasn't after your laptop or your mother's silver," James said. "They were searching for the coins, Cass. Only they found out that the coins couldn't be taken."

Cassidy was perplexed. *Who in the world would want those coins, and why?*

ဢဢဢဢဢ

On Monday, Cassidy sat on the top row of the gym bleachers, waiting for Eliza to show up for morning assembly.

"Did you call a sub in for Mr. Alita? He's out sick today."

Cassidy looked around and wondered who had spoken. All around her, the bleachers were filled with the other eighth-graders, but that had definitely been an adult talking.

On the far side of the gym, near the door to the hallway, she saw Mr. Edwards pointing out something on his clipboard to Mrs. Carmichael, the assistant principal. Cassidy's eyes widened as she clearly heard Mrs. Carmichael answer, *"Dave Rice is on his way in, but he'll be a little late. I'll cover first period until he gets here."*

Whoa, Cassidy thought. *I just heard every word they said.* Her gaze drifted down to the first row, where Luis was sitting next to his friend Brennan. *"It was too long, man. It was like the movie that wouldn't quit or something."*

Cassidy frowned. *What's going on? Did I just hear Luis talking to Brennan about a movie?* As she watched, she heard Luis's friend say, *"Cassidy Chen is totally checking you out, man."* Cassidy turned away quickly, but not before she heard Luis's answer: *"I doubt it. She's hot for this dude in our kung fu class."*

Eliza scooted in next to Cassidy on the top row. "Amazing," she said. "For once I'm five minutes early."

"Totally out of character," Cassidy agreed with a grin. "Hey, how's your hand? Does it hurt?"

"Not really," Eliza said. "My mom saw it, and I told her I scratched it on the swing. What about your arm?"

"All healed," Cassidy reported.

"What about your room?" Cassidy had called Eliza and told her about the break-in. "Did you get it cleaned up? Find anything else missing?"

"Everything's back in place—except for my laptop and my mom's silver. Oh yeah, and my grandfather's photograph."

"It's too bizarre," Eliza declared. "You fight that fox monster thing in the morning and then go home to *that.*"

"James asked me if I thought they were connected."

"Are you serious? Like, it was another demon or something that broke into your house?"

"I don't know about a demon—but maybe somebody who knows something about the coins."

"But they didn't take the coins," Eliza pointed out.

"Right, but they tore the house to pieces like they were *looking* for something specific. James thinks they were searching for the coins and then for some reason couldn't actually *take* them."

"Like they were afraid of them? Or the coins shocked them if they tried to touch them—something like that?"

Cassidy shrugged. "Maybe."

"And I guess you still don't plan on telling your parents? Come on, Cass, if somebody broke into your house, then they might do *anything* to get the coins."

"I can't tell them yet," Cassidy said. "They won't take me seriously."

"You don't know that for su—"

"Do you smell that orange?" Cassidy looked around, expecting to see someone nearby peeling a piece of fruit for a quick breakfast.

"Okay, fine, I'll change the subject," Eliza grumbled. "What orange?"

"It's, like, really strong," Cassidy said, and then she noticed a girl sitting on the top row of the seventh-grade section pop something orange into her mouth. "Over there," Cassidy said, nodding toward the other side of the gym. "That girl's eating an orange."

Eliza squinted to see what Cassidy was pointing to. "You smell *that* orange from all the way over here?" She turned and gaped at Cassidy. "What are you, like, a bloodhound now?"

"It's weird, Eliza," Cassidy told her, putting it together. "I think my senses are sort of kicked up or something. I can hear people far away talking as if they're sitting next to me. I smelled that orange like it was in front of me. I think this might be like the healing ability I got for defeating the snake demon." She swiveled and faced Eliza, a grin spreading across her face. "You know, a gift."

"That little trick could come in handy," Eliza said. "Hey, Cass, can you hear this?" Eliza stood up. *"Sing a song of sixpence,"* she sang.

"Funny, but also embarrassing," Cassidy said, glancing around. "So will you please sit down?"

But Eliza continued to sing, louder now and in a high falsetto voice so that people around her started to turn and look. *"A pocketful of rye. Four-and-twenty blackbirds baked in a pie . . ."*

"Come on, Eliza." Cassidy reached out for Eliza's arm, but Eliza pulled away and began walking down the steps toward the gym floor, still singing. *"When the pie was opened, the birds began to sing . . ."*

Cassidy watched Eliza cross to the podium that Mr. Edwards had set up on the floor. *What is she doing?* Cassidy wondered. She glanced around nervously. The rest of the students slowly stopped whatever they were doing and stared. All conversation stopped, and Eliza's voice echoed throughout the gym.

"Wasn't that a dainty dish to set before the king?" Eliza finished loudly. Then a sharp, shrill laugh burst out of her. A laugh that sounded like it belonged to an insane person. And at that moment it became all too clear to Cassidy that something was very wrong with her best friend.

🌸 Chapter Sixteen

Cassidy sat in study hall the last period of the day working on her homework. She was finding it hard to concentrate because she was listening to Erin Baker and Tyra Hume, both cheerleaders, whispering to each other several tables away.

"She's acting so totally weird," Erin said. *"Freak-out weird, you know?"*

"Yeah, like that song thing she did in assembly— embarrassing. Maybe she thinks it's funny or something, but it is so totally not funny."

"I know. I mean, what was that all about?"

Cassidy knew they were talking about Eliza,

and she fought the urge to go over and confront them. But what could she say? That Eliza was just practicing her singing? That she was doing it on a dare? And how could she explain that she heard them?

When the bell rang, Cassidy put her books in her backpack and started out of the study hall. Tyra and Erin were a few feet in front of her.

"I'm pretty sure I'm getting the new iPod for my birthday," Tyra was saying. At least they had stopped talking about Eliza.

"Cool! I would love to have the new one—you can download video!" Erin answered.

Cassidy felt a twinge of jealousy. She had wanted an iPod when they first came out, but her parents had said that it was just a fad and she should wait until the prices came down.

Tyra and Erin turned the next corner, heading toward the gym. *Cheerleading practice today,* Cassidy remembered. She had planned to go back to the playground and practice her drills again but now decided to hang around the gym and keep an eye on Eliza.

At the door to the gym, Cassidy ran into Eliza. "Hey, I thought I'd hang around during practice," Cassidy said. "Then we can walk home together."

"Sure," Eliza said, shrugging.

Cassidy walked down to a bench at the far end of the gym and took out a library book while Eliza headed off to the locker room to change.

Several minutes into the practice, Cassidy's

attention was pulled away from her book. Eliza was clapping to the same beat as the other cheerleaders, but she wasn't chanting the team cheer. Instead she was shouting: *"Patty cake, patty cake, baker's man . . ."*

Why is she doing that? Cassidy wondered.

Tamika, the squad captain, stopped the cheer and crossed her arms angrily. At once the rest of the squad turned to face Eliza.

"What?" Eliza asked innocently. "Why's everybody stopping?"

"Eliza, are you going to do this cheer or not?" Tamika demanded.

Cassidy looked across the gym at Eliza, who held her hands up in mid-clap, the red scratch visible on her right palm.

"You're wasting our time, Eliza," Tamika said. "You act like this is all just a big joke. If you're not going to be serious and do the cheer right—"

"Eliza," Coach Rogers intervened, "maybe you should take a break. Get some water and then go home early. Rest up."

Eliza looked around at the other cheerleaders, shrugged, and strolled across the floor to the locker room.

Cassidy started to follow Eliza, but Coach Rogers called out to her. "Cassidy, come with me into the office, please. Tamika, run everyone through that last cheer again."

She wants to talk about Eliza, Cassidy thought as

she followed Coach Rogers into the office. Cassidy wondered what she could say to save the situation.

"Cassidy, do you know what's going on with Eliza?" the coach asked, closing her office door. "I know you two are good friends and . . . she just hasn't been herself lately."

"Her mother's planning a move to Phoenix," Cassidy said. "Eliza really doesn't want to go."

Coach Rogers nodded. "I understand. Eliza told us about the move some time ago. But she also said that her mother might change her mind."

"Exactly," Cassidy said. "Ms. Clifford's talked about moving before, but I think this time Eliza feels she'll really do it."

"That's too bad. I know that a move can be very upsetting, but . . . well, you saw what she was doing out there," the coach said. "Do you think something else could be going on?"

"I don't know," Cassidy admitted. "I'm going to go talk to her, though."

"I hope it will help," the coach said. "Eliza's a great girl, full of energy and life. She's a terrific cheerleader, and we really don't want to lose her."

Cassidy nodded and headed out to find her friend. When she got to the locker room, she started to push open the door—and then stopped. Eliza was inside talking to someone. Had one of the other cheerleaders followed her in?

"Did you see their faces? They were acting like

I was running naked through the gym with my hair on fire. They have no sense of humor."

Cassidy waited but didn't hear anyone else speak, so she pushed open the door and walked in. Eliza sat on one end of a bench, and she was alone. "Hey, Cass," she said. "I guess we get to leave early."

"Right." Cassidy cast around for a tactful way to begin and decided there wasn't one. "Um . . . so what happened out there?"

"Nothing happened," Eliza told her. "Except that some people can't take a joke."

"The 'patty-cake' thing?" Cassidy asked. "Was that supposed to be a joke?" Eliza had always been so serious about cheerleading. None of this made any sense. *Eliza's not herself!* Cassidy realized.

"Everything's cool." Eliza shrugged. "Let's get out of here."

෨ ෨ ෨ ෨ ෨

Back at her apartment, Eliza asked Cassidy to come up and look at some clothes she'd found at Tootie's Vintage Tees. Eliza put the key in the lock and swung the door in, but it didn't open all the way.

"That's weird," Eliza said. She and Cassidy squeezed through the narrow opening and saw what had blocked the door. Several boxes were stacked head high and labeled "Kitchen Stuff."

Cassidy's eyes flicked to Eliza, who had turned

pale. "Unbelievable," Eliza muttered. "She's already started packing!"

Eliza threw the keys down on the table and noticed the blinking light of the answering machine. She hit the button, and a woman's chirpy voice sang out, *"Hellooo, Ms. Clifford, this is Rita with Sun Realty. Just wanted to let you know the Levines are considering your offer! You're going to absolutely love it here in Phoenix!"*

In about two seconds flat Eliza's face went from stark white to rage red. "This is seriously messed up!" she shouted.

"I'm calling the Happy Bunny," Cassidy said, alarmed. "I'll stay with you until your mom gets home."

But Cassidy wasn't even sure that Eliza had heard her. She was already inside her room, slamming the door behind her. Cassidy pulled out her cell and made a quick call to her mom, explaining that Eliza was upset and she wanted to stay with her awhile.

Cassidy took a deep breath and walked toward Eliza's room. She knocked lightly on the door. "Eliza, can I come in?" There was no answer. "Eliza, I'm coming in. Let's talk about this, okay?"

Cassidy pushed open the door and found Eliza standing at the edge of her bed holding a pair of scissors. She yanked a pair of green cords from a pile of clothes on her bed and began cutting. On the floor Cassidy saw several ragged scraps of fabric, bright pink wool, dark denim, purple fleece.

❧ *Chapter Seventeen*

"What are you doing?" Cassidy exclaimed.

Eliza continued cutting the pants into a pile of rags. "I won't need these in Phoenix," she said. Her voice sounded strangely bright and cheerful. "Grab a pair of scissors, Cass, you can help me!"

"Come on, Eliza, don't do this," Cassidy said. "Just put down the scissors and let's talk."

Eliza picked up one of her favorite sweatshirts and made savage cuts in the sleeves with the scissors. "Won't need sleeves in Phoenix! Won't need long pants! Let's cut them all off! I'm going to absolutely *love* it in Phoenix!" she cried, mimicking the realtor's chirpy tone.

"Please, Eliza, just stop it for a minute," Cassidy pleaded. "Stop!"

Eliza froze. She stared at the ruined clothes scattered around the bed and floor and shook her head, suddenly looking confused. "Why did I do that?" she asked. "I mean — *why*?"

Eliza sank onto the edge of the bed and began scratching her palm. Cassidy walked over to her and sat down beside her.

"What's wrong with your hand?" Cassidy asked.

"It's itching like crazy," Eliza replied, showing Cassidy the diagonal red slash she had on her palm. The wound looked as red and fresh as it had when it first happened. *It should have started healing by now,* Cassidy thought, wondering if the cut was infected.

"Eliza? I'm ho-ome," announced Sarah Clifford in a singsong voice.

"I'm going to talk to your mom," Cassidy told Eliza. "Just stay in here and . . . and don't cut up any more clothes, okay?"

Eliza didn't look up — she just nodded and continued scratching her palm.

Sarah Clifford smiled when she saw Cassidy come into the living room. "Hello, Cassidy, I didn't know you were coming over."

"I . . . uh, I walked home with Eliza," Cassidy said. "Ms. Clifford, could I talk to you about something?"

"Sure, Cass," Ms. Clifford said. "Is everything all right? Is Eliza okay?"

"Well . . . to be honest . . . she's really upset about the move," Cassidy began.

"Oh, the move!" Sarah Clifford said, interrupting. "I know it'll be an adjustment for her, but I'm sure she'll love it once she gets there. Eliza makes friends easily, and she has cousins there, too. You'll have to come visit as soon as we get settled."

Cassidy realized that Eliza's mother had no idea how upsetting this was for her daughter. "I guess Eliza doesn't see it that way. When we got back here today, she saw the moving boxes and then there was a message from a realtor on the phone . . ."

Sarah Clifford made a little *tsk* sound. "I expected to be home before she got here. I thought she had practice after school today."

"Yeah, well, the coach sent her home early," Cassidy said. "I guess she could tell how down in the dumps Eliza was. She's back in her room . . . cutting up some of her clothes."

Eliza's mother frowned. "Cutting up her clothes? Is she really that upset about the move, or is she just being dramatic?"

"She's really, really upset," Cassidy said again, feeling that she wasn't getting through.

"Thanks, Cassidy," Sarah Clifford said. "I better go see how she's doing. I have just the thing to cheer her up—I'm going to fly her down to Phoenix this week. When she sees how warm and sunny it is there, I'm sure she'll change her mind."

Cassidy was exhausted by the time she got home from Eliza's and found her mom sitting at the kitchen table, looking through the mail.

"I got a strange phone call from the police today," Wendy said as Cassidy poured a glass of milk. "They found your laptop in a Dumpster downtown."

"In a Dumpster?" Cassidy sat at the table across from her mom. "I thought they said somebody probably stole it to sell. Quick money and all that."

"I know. It's really very odd," her mother told her. "They found the silver, too. Well, not all the pieces, but the police said it looked as if it had all just been dumped in there."

"So, if the thieves didn't even want the stuff they stole, then why did they take it?" Cassidy asked.

"The police suspect that they took the stuff to cover up what they were really after and then didn't want to run the risk of being caught pawning it."

"But they didn't take anything else—except for the picture, and that makes no sense either," Cassidy told her.

"None of it makes sense," her mother agreed. "Your dad's worried that whoever broke in didn't find what they were looking for and might come back."

Cassidy thought about what James had said. That maybe they wanted the coins but discovered they couldn't take them. She wondered if they'd be back to try again.

"Anyway, I'd say your laptop's probably ruined," her mom continued. "The police think it's been in the Dumpster for days. Besides, the officer said they need to keep everything for evidence—for a while, at least."

"So am I going to get a new laptop? I need one for homework," Cassidy said.

Wendy frowned. "I think the insurance company will reimburse us. It may be a while, though. You'll have to use the computer in your dad's office until then."

Cassidy wasn't happy about having to use her father's computer. Getting her own laptop had been her Christmas gift the year before. She liked to e-mail and IM with her friends in the evening. When she used her dad's computer, he pretty much limited her to homework or research for school.

"Dad's home," Cassidy said absently, thinking that she might ask him if they could go ahead and start looking for a new laptop right away. She had seen one in a sales flyer that was perfect.

Wendy glanced toward the window, then back at the mail. "You're hearing things, Cass."

But Cassidy had been certain that she'd heard her dad's car—she thought she'd even heard music from the country-western radio station that he liked to listen to. A few moments later Simon made the turn up the long driveway that led to the garage.

Wendy looked at Cassidy and frowned. "You heard him from—where?—down the street?"

Cassidy just smiled at her mother. "Dad's radio," she said. "He plays it kind of loud."

"*I* didn't hear it," Wendy said.

"You know what they say, Mom," Cassidy teased. "The hearing's always the first to go."

"Yeah, very funny," her mother said, slitting the last of the envelopes.

Cassidy met her father as he opened the door to the kitchen. "Hi, Dad, I need to use your computer. I have a paper due."

Her father smiled and shook his head. "Yes, well, it's so good to see you, too. And my day was just fine, thank you."

"Sorry," Cassidy said, giggling. "So, your day was good . . . That's good . . ."

"Oh, now she's patronizing me," her father said. He put his briefcase down on a chair and kissed his wife on the forehead. "Hello, dear."

But Wendy didn't answer. She was looking at a piece of mail and frowning.

"Fine, Cassidy," her dad told her. "You may use my computer—but no new screen savers, no games. I like the settings just the way I have them—no *meows* or *yippees* when I open files or check e-mail."

Cassidy laughed and promised her dad that she wouldn't change anything. As she started out of the room, her mother called back to her, "Whoa, there, wait just a minute."

"What, Mom?" Cassidy asked.

"I'm trying to understand a very unusual purchase on my credit card bill," her mother said.

Cassidy walked over to the table and looked at the paper her mother held in her hands. "Right here," Wendy said. "A pair of jeans from VibeBuy—a *two-hundred-and-fifteen-dollar* pair of jeans from VibeBuy."

Cassidy stared at the charge on the credit card bill and then back at her mother. "You don't think I charged the jeans on your card, do you?"

"Well, *I* certainly didn't buy them. It's not exactly my kind of shop, Cass. And you were just telling me the other day how much you wanted those jeans."

"Mom!" Cassidy cried. "Sure, I wanted them, but I wouldn't take your card and charge something like that."

Simon came to the table, and Wendy handed him the bill.

He frowned. "Is it possible that you bought the jeans as a gift for Cassidy and then maybe you just forgot?"

"Absolutely not!" Wendy snapped. "Don't you think I'd remember spending over two hundred dollars on a pair of jeans?"

"Well, I'd remember, too, Mom," Cassidy protested. "I didn't do it."

"Okay, everybody just calm down," Simon said. "I'm sure there's an explanation."

"If you don't believe me, search my room," Cassidy said, crossing her arms over her chest.

Her mother was silent. "Well, if neither one of us bought the jeans, then how do you explain the charge?" she asked at last.

As Cassidy combed her brain for an answer to her mother's question, she absentmindedly fixed her gaze on her reflection in the window over the kitchen sink. As she watched, her image wavered, flickered, and then reappeared. Only now the image she saw in the dark panes of glass was laughing maniacally.

Cassidy's mouth dropped open. The reflection taunted her with an evil wink and then faded away, leaving Cassidy's own frightened reflection looking back.

"I honestly don't know," Cassidy said.

❧ *Chapter Eighteen*

The next Wednesday during Wing Chun class, Cassidy was paired with a new student for kicking drills. He had about six inches and eighty pounds on Cassidy, but her skills had improved so much that she had to be careful not to kick the pad too hard and hurt him.

Master Lau watched the pair for a while and then took the pad from Cassidy's kicking partner. "Now, Cassidy," he said, "you may actually kick and use all your power."

Cassidy felt a little embarrassed. The new student turned beet red and stepped back as Master

Lau positioned the kicking pad in place over his own chest.

Cassidy went through the drills she had been practicing in the abandoned playground. She delivered a strong kick to the center of the pad, retreated, turned, and kicked again with perfect precision. Then she looked at Master Lau's face. It registered nothing, but Cassidy knew that the kick had been fierce.

"Well done, Cassidy," the *shifu* said. He bowed slightly after removing the kicking pad. As Master Lau walked back to the front of the room, Cassidy glanced toward Luis and James. Luis smiled and gave her a thumbs-up, but James was just looking down at the floor.

At the end of class Master Lau called the students together for an announcement. Luis found his way to Cassidy's side as they gathered closer to their teacher.

Master Lau looked around at each of the students who stood before him. "I have chosen four students from this class to participate in the tournament in Hong Kong."

Cassidy felt the warmth of Luis's arm next to her. From the corner of her eye she saw that James stood several steps away at the far edge of the group.

"Each of the participants who are invited to compete will be expected to work hard in preparation for the competition," Master Lau continued. "I may also ask the participants to meet with me for one-on-

one lessons."

Master Lau paused and looked at the students again. "This path will not be easy," he continued. "If you are chosen and you feel in your heart that you cannot be serious about what is to come, then I would ask you to do the honorable thing and bow out."

Cassidy could almost feel Luis's anticipation as he stood next to her. Then she glanced at James, his face giving away nothing.

"And now, I ask everyone to receive my selections with proper restraint and respect."

Cassidy could almost hear the beat of her own heart as she nervously wiped sweaty palms against her pants.

"Luis Alvarez," Master Lau announced.

Cassidy glanced at Luis and smiled. He nodded slightly, but Cassidy knew that inside he was holding back a full-on seizure.

"Majesta Madison," Lau continued. Majesta let out a barely audible squeal, followed by a small, "Sorry."

Master Lau continued, "Cassidy Chen . . ." He looked at her as he called her name and gave a slight nod. She hadn't realized that she had been holding her breath until a tiny sigh escaped her lips. Even though she knew how strong her skills had become, it was a relief to hear her name called.

I'm going to Hong Kong! I'm really, really going to Hong Kong! Her heart leaped with excitement, but respecting her teacher's wishes, she stood still and betrayed no emotion.

There was only one name left to be called. Cassidy silently prayed it'd be the right one.

"And finally . . . James Tang."

Thank goodness it's James! Cassidy stole a look at James, who hadn't moved a muscle. *Isn't he excited? Doesn't he understand what an incredible honor this is?*

"I will have packets of information about this trip for your parents by next week," Master Lau said. "If you have any questions, you may see me in my office." He turned quickly and walked away from the students.

The door to Master Lau's office closed, and Luis whirled around and grabbed Cassidy in a huge hug. "We're going to Hong Kong!" he cried.

"I know. We made it!" she said, unable to conceal her own delight.

Majesta walked over to them. "This is showing restraint?"

Luis released Cassidy with a laugh. "Oh, get over yourself, Majesta," he said. "I heard you squeal. You're excited, too. Besides, Master Lau just meant to show restraint *in his presence.*"

"Looks like James and I will have to act as chaperones for you and Cassidy on this trip," Majesta said.

James and I? Cassidy cringed at the sound of it. And what was Majesta implying anyway—that

Cassidy and Luis were a couple? Cassidy wished that *something* would keep Majesta from going on this trip. *Nothing too horrible,* she thought, *maybe a sore throat, an ear infection, a sprained wrist.*

As James walked over to the group, he nodded his thanks to a few students who hung back after class to offer their congratulations.

"James," Majesta began when he joined them, "didn't I tell you that you should go ahead and pack your bags? I knew you'd be picked."

"I'm not sure I'll be going," James answered.

"But why wouldn't you go?" Luis asked. "This is big!"

"Yeah, it's big for Lau," James answered. "He wants to look like some hotshot—and he knows that *we'll* make him look good."

Luis scowled. "Master Lau's not like that. You don't know him." James just shrugged and walked away. "What a jerk," Luis said. "We'd probably be better off if he didn't go—especially if he's gonna be like that. He'll bring down the whole team."

"He's better than all of us," Majesta said as she flipped her long, silky dark hair away from her face. "We might, and I stress *might,* be able to win a few individual competitions. But without James, there's no way we'll win any of the team events."

"And Master Lau knows that," Luis added. "Which is probably the *only* reason he picked James anyway."

"I think James will go," Cassidy said. "He'll do it for the rest of us."

"I'll talk to him." Majesta smiled—her teeth perfect and toothpaste white. "I think he'll listen to me." She walked away and followed James out the door.

Luis turned to Cassidy. "You know what?" he said. "I don't care if either one of them goes."

Cassidy didn't say anything, but she cared very much. She really wanted James to go. *Maybe I can find out more about my grandfather in Hong Kong—more about my ancestors and the coins, too. James can help me with that.*

But she had to admit that the real reason she wanted James Tang on the trip was that she simply wanted to spend more time with him.

Chapter Nineteen

Cassidy's heart thumped a little harder than usual as she dialed James later that evening. This was an important call, and she hoped it would go well.

"Hey, James, it's Cassidy," she said when he picked up. "You got a minute?"

"Sure, what's up?" James asked.

"I just wondered if you really meant it—that you might not go to Hong Kong with us."

"Did Majesta tell you to call me?" he asked.

"Majesta?" Cassidy repeated, confused.

"Majesta called, like, just a few minutes ago, right before you did. She's all over me about going to Hong Kong—what a great opportunity it is, how much fun we'll have. Blah blah blah."

"Well, it *will* be fun—but no, Majesta didn't ask me to call you," Cassidy said. "I just wanted to tell you that I really hope you go with us. I mean, we all do—the whole team." Cassidy was careful to not make this too personal. *Keep it light,* she had instructed herself before calling.

"I'm considering it, okay?" James said. "But it's not *me* that the team needs. It's you, Cass, *you're* the team. You could win every event, probably with your eyes closed! Maybe the others haven't noticed how good you are, but I have."

If he's saying what I think he's saying, that must mean he watches me, Cassidy thought, her heart fluttering a little. *I wish I knew if he was trying to tell me something.*

"Thanks, James," Cassidy said, grateful that they were on the phone, because she felt her face flushing. "But really—"

"You actually *fight* demons, Cass," James added. "Do you realize how amazing that is? You actually *use* your skills. The rest of us just practice."

Cassidy didn't know what to say. She was thrilled to hear James say that—but what did it mean, really? Some of the time he treated her like a kid sister. Other times he seemed to be flirting with her. And now *this*—how was she supposed to know how he really felt? *Are all boys this hard to figure out?* she wondered.

"So how did Eliza handle seeing you fight the

fox demon?" James asked. "Did it totally freak her out, or is she pretty cool with it?"

"I wouldn't say she's cool with it," Cassidy said. "It makes me sick that she got hurt. The fox scratched her pretty badly."

"On the hand, right? Sounds harsh."

"Yeah—it could have been a lot worse, though. Right now Eliza's got other problems, and I guess the stress is making her do some crazy stuff—crazy even for Eliza." She told James about Eliza's odd behavior at school and cutting up her clothes.

"It sounds like that kung fu movie about the two brothers," James said. "I can't remember the title, but one brother gets bitten by a fox and it makes him crazy. He's some kind of fighter in this village, and then he gets cursed by the fox's bite and he tears his hair out, scratches his face to pieces—it's pretty gross."

"I never saw that one," Cassidy said—and from the description she was glad she hadn't. "But what are you saying—that Eliza might be cursed by the fox's scratch?"

"I don't know. Maybe," James said. "Or, like you say, maybe it's just the family stuff that's making her kind of nuts."

"Hmm." Cassidy thought this over. Eliza had been through the moving drama with her mother many times before, and she'd never acted like this.

"So what happened in the movie?" Cassidy asked. "How did they cure the guy who gets cursed?"

The pause was unmistakable. In fact, Cassidy wondered for a minute if the phone connection had gone dead. "James?" she asked. "Are you there?"

"Yeah, I'm here," James said. "It was just a movie, Cass."

"I know. So what did they do? How did they save the guy?"

She felt nervous when she heard him take in a deep breath, as if he were preparing to give her bad news. "They couldn't save him," he said finally. "His brother had to put him out of his misery."

"He killed him?" Cassidy squeaked.

"A *movie*, Cassidy," James said quickly. "That's all it was."

"Yeah, but what if—" Cassidy couldn't even finish the sentence. This was horrible. The fox demon might have been the one to scratch Eliza, but Eliza wouldn't have been out there if it hadn't been for Cassidy. If Eliza was going crazy now—

"Listen to me," James said. "I'm sure there's nothing to this, okay? I shouldn't have mentioned it."

"But James, you should see the scratch," Cassidy said, remembering Eliza sitting in the middle of the scraps of clothes, scratching her palm. "It's not really healing—it looks—kind of *bad*."

"Let's do this," James said. "You keep an eye on Eliza, see if there's anything else out of the ordinary, and I'll do some research."

"I guess . . ." What else could Cassidy say? It

wasn't like she had any other ideas.

"Are you okay?" he asked.

"Yeah, I'm okay," Cassidy said. "I'm just worried."

"We'll figure it out, I promise," James said. "I'll e-mail you if I find anything."

"Thanks, James," Cassidy said.

As Cassidy snapped her phone closed, she thought about Eliza in Phoenix and wondered whether she was okay.

Cassidy decided to take a hot shower. It had been a long day, and she was exhausted. She hoped the hot water and steam would help her feel better.

As the mist swirled about her, Cassidy tried to figure out what she should do about Eliza.

The movie was just a movie—that's all, she reminded herself. *Eliza's just really upset right now and she's trying to get her mother's attention.*

But another thought nagged her. Sarah Clifford probably didn't even know how weird Eliza had been acting at school—so how was *that* supposed to get her mother's attention?

Cassidy forced herself to face the other possibility. *What if Eliza is cursed? If the fox demon did something to her, then I've got to figure out how to undo it. Maybe I'll ask Master Lau.*

As Cassidy stepped out of the shower and began to dry off, something across the room caught her eye. She glanced at the fogged mirror and blinked, trying

"Okay, I get it," Eliza said. "It's embarrassing. I don't know *why* I did that stuff—or the things in Phoenix, either. I don't *know* why!"

Eliza was silent. *She hates me,* Cassidy thought. *And she has every right to hate me. Maybe it would be better for Eliza if she did move to Phoenix and just got away from me.*

"It'll be okay. We'll go to Master Lau," Cassidy told her. "He knows all about Chinese mysticism. Maybe he can help you."

"Like how?" Eliza asked, panic rising in her voice. "By performing some kind of *exorcist* thing? No thanks. What if he makes it all worse?"

"I think it's worth a shot, Eliza. It's not like we have any better options at this point. Just say you'll meet me at the studio tomorrow."

Eliza reluctantly agreed, and they said goodbye. As Cassidy flipped her cell phone closed, it slipped out of her hand and slid under her dresser. When she crouched down to look for it, she saw a dark piece of clothing under the dresser. She pulled it out and stared at it.

It was the jeans—the totally cool, insanely expensive jeans from VibeBuy.

Chapter Twenty-One

Cassidy quickly closed the door to her room. She rolled the jeans up tightly and hid them between a stack of sweatshirts in her dresser. *I can't let Mom see these!* she thought frantically.

Just as Cassidy shut the drawer, there was a light tap at her door. Wendy peeked her head in and handed Cassidy the cordless phone. "Phone call," she said, and then mouthed the words, *It's a boy.*

Did she see? Cassidy wondered nervously as she silently vowed to get rid of the jeans tomorrow.

Cassidy took the phone from her mother. Wendy winked once and smiled, then left the room, closing the door behind her.

"Hello?" Cassidy said.

"Hey, you," James said. "You screening?"

Cassidy looked at her cell phone on the floor and frowned. "Uh, no, but I dropped my phone before. It must have fallen on the Power button."

"I wondered if you'd heard from Eliza," James said. "And I also wanted to tell you something else."

"What?"

"I'm going to Hong Kong, but I'm *not* doing it for Master Lau or anything like that. I'm doing it for you and Majesta . . . and even Luis."

"That's great," Cassidy said, her heart pounding with excitement. She remembered the words from James's mother on her foggy mirror. *She must have found a way to get through to him,* Cassidy thought. "I'm really glad. I mean, the whole team will be happy."

"Majesta thinks she talked me into it," James said.

That means he called Majesta first, Cassidy realized with a pang. For the hundredth time, she wondered why Majesta Madison had to be part of her life.

"Well, did she?" Cassidy asked, not sure she wanted to know the answer.

"Not really," James admitted. "I just decided on my own. My dad's really happy about it, too."

Cassidy smiled to herself. So was she.

"Anyway," James continued. "I wanted to tell you that—but also check on Eliza."

Cassidy told him about what had happened in Phoenix and the strange e-mail she'd received from Eliza. She explained that she'd finally convinced Eliza that they needed to see Master Lau after class the next day.

"You really think he can help?" James sounded skeptical.

"I don't know. I hope so."

"Well, for your friend's sake, I hope so, too. But there's just something about Lau that—"

Cassidy sighed. "What, James? What is this *something* about Master Lau that you don't like?"

"I just don't trust him." James said. "And I guess he kind of reminds me of my Wing Chun teacher in Hong Kong. Another hotshot, just like Lau."

"Speaking of trust," Cassidy said, "my mom's beginning to think that somebody got her credit card number and is out there committing identity theft."

"Yeah, well, maybe that did happen. Someone *did* break into your house."

"The question is whether the person who broke into my house is the same person who left the two-hundred-dollar pair of jeans in my *room*," she added, quickly explaining about the mysterious charge on her mom's card and the pair of jeans under her dresser.

"Very weird," James agreed. "I hate to say this, but maybe Eliza did it. You know . . . because of the fox demon scratch . . ."

Cassidy thought about this a minute. Was that

possible? If so, it wouldn't have really been Eliza's fault, since she wouldn't have really known what she was doing.

"I guess that's possible," Cassidy said at last. "But somehow that doesn't feel right to me."

⊘⊘⊘⊘⊘

After they got off the phone, Cassidy lay back on her bed and stared at the ceiling. *Could my life get any more complicated?* Then she caught herself. *My life* will *get more complicated. There are two more coins left. Which means two more demons.* One of which she suspected had something to do with those mirror images.

She sat straight up on her bed. Suddenly everything was beginning to add up. The *reflection* wore those VibeBuy jeans. That meant there was no way Eliza was involved—and made it very likely that something demonic was actually going on.

Cassidy made sure that Monty wasn't in her room, took out the coins, and examined the one with four marks on the back. This would be the next demon.

The engraving showed a woman holding a sword in front of her, point up. Only one side of the woman's face was visible. The other half was hidden behind the sword's blade.

So what kind of demon does this represent? Cassidy wondered. *And does the woman's face have anything to do with my strange reflection?*

❧ Chapter Twenty-Two

Cassidy was elated to see Eliza waiting for her the next day after Wing Chun class. Cassidy knew how nervous Eliza was about seeing Master Lau and half expected that she wouldn't even show up.

"I *really* don't like this," Eliza whispered to Cassidy as they walked to the *shifu's* door. "But I hope he can do something."

Cassidy gave Eliza's hand what she hoped was a reassuring squeeze. *I hope it works, too,* she thought. *Because I don't know if we have any other options.*

"Master Lau," Cassidy said. "This is my friend Eliza, the one I told you about."

"Please have a seat," Master Lau said in his polite, formal tone.

Eliza was visibly nervous but sat down. Master Lau observed her closely. "Is that a scratch on your palm?" he asked.

Eliza nodded.

"May I look at it?" Master Lau's forehead creased, and his eyes were darker than usual.

Eliza held up her palm.

"This is very troubling," Master Lau said.

He almost looks . . . frightened, Cassidy realized. Seeing his fear, Cassidy grew even more anxious.

"I think it is possible," he said, "that something is using your spirit."

"*Using* my spirit?" Eliza said. "Like—like a *possession*?"

Master Lau hesitated; he seemed to be choosing his words carefully. "It's possible for certain types of . . . let's just say, *dark* spirits, to take over the spirit of another. This may be permanent, or it may be temporary. It's always dangerous."

"You mean I might be like this forever," Eliza said, her voice bleak.

"We need to force out the unwanted spirit," Master Lau said gently. "I'm curious, however." This time Master Lau looked directly at Cassidy. "Do you have any idea how something like this could happen to your friend? It's not very common in these times."

"Not a clue," Cassidy said, hoping she sounded

believable. She glanced at Eliza, who frowned at her. Cassidy sent her a silent plea. *Please don't mention the fox demon.* "But Eliza's been pretty upset about some things going on at home."

"I see," Master Lau said, in a way that made Cassidy wonder if he knew something was up. "Well, let's see what we can do."

Master Lau moved a small table in front of Eliza and then placed a thick red candle on top. Before lighting the candle, he took a small vial of oil from a shelf behind his desk. Carefully he poured three small drops onto the yellow wick. When he lit the candle, it sputtered and then sent a thin dark plume of smoke curling into the air.

The smell was sweet, almost too sweet. It hung in the air, reminding Cassidy of rotting fruit.

Cassidy wondered what he was doing, but she didn't want to interrupt him with questions.

Eliza was usually a lively chatterbox, but she also sat very still and quiet in her chair. Cassidy knew that her friend was afraid and nervous. But Eliza had been so tormented that Cassidy was sure she'd do almost anything to feel better. Eliza held her hands in her lap as she stared at the yellow flame of the flickering candle.

Now Master Lau held a tiny brass bell that he rang next to Eliza's right ear and then her left. Its sound was pure and clear, and when Eliza heard it, she closed her eyes and her face completely relaxed, almost as if she were asleep.

Master Lau began chanting in a soft low tone that was almost impossible to hear. *What's he saying?* Cassidy wondered. *Is he actually calling out to whatever dark spirit is inside Eliza? Can it really be the fox demon?*

Master Lau walked around Eliza's chair slowly, chanting, moving his hands over her without touching her.

He stopped abruptly and leaned in close to her ear. "Eliza, I want you to blow out the candle now," he told her. "I command the dark spirit to leave you."

Cassidy watched as Eliza leaned forward, eyes still closed. As she blew out the candle, Cassidy was astounded to see a smoky gray spirit leave Eliza's body and hover over the candle flame. The candle sputtered, spitting bright sparks into the room. The flame grew larger and then small again before going out with a dying hiss.

Eliza slumped in her seat and the color drained from her face. Cassidy looked toward Master Lau — but he, too, seemed to be in a trance. He stood with his hands outstretched over the candle, the flame completely extinguished. His eyes were closed and he was breathing deeply, taking in the last of the wispy smoke rising up from the dark wick of the candle. Just as he dropped his hands to his sides and opened his eyes, Cassidy saw Eliza, as pale as death, begin to fall from the chair.

Chapter Twenty-Three

With lightning reflexes, the *shifu* caught Eliza's falling body. Gently he straightened her in her chair. Eliza's eyes remained shut, and Cassidy could barely see her breathing.

"Eliza!" Cassidy cried. "Eliza, wake up!"

Master Lau waved a scented cloth in front of Eliza's nose, and her eyes began to flutter open.

"Is she all right?" Cassidy asked. "What happened?"

"She'll be fine," Master Lau said. "Eliza, how do you feel now?"

Eliza took a deep breath. "I'm okay," she said.

"I mean, I feel a lot better."

Cassidy felt herself trembling with relief and happiness. "Master Lau, thank you so much. I'm so glad we came to you. I don't know what would have happened if—"

"I'm glad I could help," he interrupted her. "Still, I'm very curious about this spirit sickness."

"Is that what it was?" Cassidy asked. "A spirit sickness?"

"Most definitely," Master Lau answered. "Eliza's had contact with a very evil spirit. My guess is he left her with a—with a remnant, you might say—of himself."

He turned to Eliza. "I'm wondering just *how* you might have come in contact with such a thing?"

Cassidy looked at Eliza, urging her with her eyes not to say anything about the fox demon.

"I don't know, Master Lau. An evil spirit—it all sounds so scary." Eliza gave a little shudder. "I'm really glad you were able to help me."

Master Lau nodded and kept his eyes on Eliza, but said nothing. Cassidy suddenly felt wary; she recognized what her teacher was doing.

A pause is like an empty bowl that wishes to be filled, he had once told his students. *When there is a pause in fighting, one opponent will become uncomfortable and make a hasty move—to fill the empty bowl. This move is usually not well thought out, and it will be costly. It is the same in important conversation. One speaker will become uncomfortable with the pause and will begin to fill the empty bowl. Often the words that pour into the bowl will not be well thought out. They may even be secrets that should remain guarded.*

Cassidy wasn't about to fill the empty bowl. She knew she needed to guard her secrets carefully. To her immense relief, Eliza seemed to know this, too.

"Thanks, Master Lau," Eliza said as she got up to leave. "If I come up with anything, I'll be sure to tell you."

ᘒᘒᘒᘒᘒ

On the bus ride home, Eliza asked why Cassidy hadn't been more honest with Master Lau. "I think the fewer people I involve in this, the better," Cassidy explained. "Look what happened to you."

"That's exactly my point. Would you just stop and think for a minute about how crazy—no, how *dangerous*—this is! I mean, I've been acting like a lunatic these last few days. It's been humiliating. But at least I wasn't hurt. Imagine if I had been injured!" Eliza said, her tone clearly conveying how frustrated she was.

"I know it's dangerous, Eliza," Cassidy said. "But what do you expect me to do? I'm sorry you got hurt—I'm *really* sorry."

"You *have* to tell someone about this. Someone who can do something about it. Master Lau helped me; what makes you so sure he can't help you?"

"There's just too much at stake," Cassidy said, noticing that their words were taking on the rough edge of an argument—an argument that she didn't want. "Let's not . . . fight, okay? I have to handle this on my own. I know you don't understand, but can you at least trust me?"

"Actually, I don't know," Eliza said, looking straight ahead. She swiveled in her seat and glared at Cassidy. "Don't you get it? Because of you, I had to . . . I've just been, like, *exorcised.*" She turned back around and gripped the seat in front of her as the bus came to a stop. "This is becoming more and more dangerous. And the only thing that seems to matter to you is hanging on to those stupid coins and fighting this crazy battle."

Before Cassidy could respond or stop her, Eliza stood and got off the bus. "Eliza, wait—" Cassidy charged toward the door, but the bus lurched, and she stumbled before the doors closed.

Cassidy settled into a seat and peered out the window of the bus. There was Eliza, waiting at the bus stop, shifting her weight from foot to foot. Cassidy couldn't tell if her friend's constant movement was an attempt to stay warm or an energy fueled by anger. Either way, she hoped that one day Eliza would understand Cassidy's choices a little better.

As the bus left Eliza behind, Cassidy remembered the two women who appeared to her in a dream on her birthday, Ng Mui and Wing Chun. *Being a warrior is a lonely fate,* one of them had said.

And now I think I know why, Cassidy thought.

@@@@@

In her room the next day Cassidy sat at her desk, wishing her father would get off his computer. She needed to talk to James about the fourth coin. But his line was busy, and he wasn't answering his cell. *He's probably talking to Majesta,* Cassidy thought, feeling the familiar pang of jealousy and anger that almost *any* thought of Majesta brought. If only she still had her laptop, she could try to reach him online.

Cassidy looked at her shrine. "Please help," she said aloud. "Please help me figure this out." She picked up the carved comb and the little jade dog charm and held them in her hands. "Can you tell me what the next demon is going to be?"

There was a light knock on her door and her mom stepped inside. "Can I talk to you a minute?"

"Uh, sure," Cassidy said. She hoped this wasn't going to be about the jeans again. She had managed to sneak them out of the house and drop them off at a homeless shelter near school. But the whole episode created a lot of tension between Cassidy and her mom—and Cassidy was ready for it all to go away.

Wendy sat on the edge of Cassidy's bed. "I owe you an apology," she said. "I've been dealing with the credit card company about that false charge. Well, according to the time and date, there's no way you could have been at VibeBuy at the time the jeans were purchased. You were in school."

Cassidy was flooded with a feeling of relief. It had been a horrible feeling—knowing that her own mom wasn't sure if she could trust her. "I told you," Cassidy said.

Wendy reached out and stroked Cassidy's face. "I know you did, kiddo, and I'm sorry. I jumped to a conclusion, which is never a good thing." Wendy stood up. "So are we good here?"

Cassidy smiled. "Yeah, Mom. We're cool."

"Good," Wendy said with a grin. "Now I can get back to nagging you about the usual things. Picking up your room, eating your fruits and vegetables . . ." Wendy winked and shut the door behind her.

Fruits and vegetables. For some reason, the words echoed in Cassidy's mind. She stared at her door, trying to figure out why.

It was *fruit*, she realized, remembering the peculiar smell she'd noticed in her room after the house was broken into. Yesterday the oil that Master Lau dripped on the candlewick gave off that same distinct odor—the smell of rotting fruit.

The scent of Master Lau's oil was in my house. Does that mean he's the one who broke in? Cassidy asked herself. She shook her head. *But that's crazy. Why would he do that?*

Chapter Twenty-Four

"What's that smell?" Cassidy asked the next morning. She noticed it immediately.

Her mother looked around the kitchen and sniffed. "Smell?"

The same as in my room and at Master Lau's. It's sweet and—

Wendy reached into a bowl of fruit on the table. "This?" She held up an orange that looked a little overripe. "Still firm—it's not too far gone."

She tossed it to Cassidy, who caught it and held it to her nose.

Yeah, that's it, Cassidy realized, feeling foolish.

She'd been getting a little carried away with this hyped-up sense thing. What if the smell in her room had been orange peels or a peach pit in her wastebasket? She couldn't believe she actually thought Master Lau might have —

"Oh, before you leave, Cass," Wendy said, interrupting Cassidy's train of thought. "Master Lau talked to your dad this morning. He wants to schedule the private lessons with you."

"When?" Cassidy asked, peeling the orange, breathing in the sweet citrus smell.

"For now he'd like to meet with you on Mondays after school," her mother said. "But he said he may ask for more time later on."

"What about the Happy Bunny?" Cassidy asked. "Usually I help out at the preschool on Mondays. I'm still trying to save up for jeans, remember?"

Wendy gave Cassidy a rueful smile. "I remember. But can we not mention jeans for just a little while?"

Cassidy laughed. "Sure, Mom. But do you think we can talk about them before I'm walking around in a pair that don't even reach my knees?"

"I think we can manage that," Wendy promised with a grin.

ⓢ ⓢ ⓢ ⓢ ⓢ

The next Monday evening Cassidy walked into the empty studio. She figured Master Lau was still in his office, so she headed toward the locker room, her shoes making hollow *thwacks* on the wood floor that reverberated around the cement walls of the gym.

As she changed into her Wing Chun clothes—a soft black T-shirt and black sweatpants—she realized that she felt a little nervous. *Of course you're nervous*, she said to herself. *This is, like, the honor of a lifetime! Private training with probably the best teacher in all of Seattle!*

She took a deep breath, walked out to the center of the studio, and stood waiting for her teacher. Thoughts swirled in her mind, but her senses were keen, and when Master Lau's hand turned the doorknob, she heard it even before the door swung open.

The *shifu* smiled briefly as he walked across the floor and faced her. They bowed solemnly, acknowledging their respect for each other, and Cassidy felt bad for ever doubting him.

"Today's lesson is about being quiet," Master Lau said. He went on to explain that much of their training together would be mental and spiritual, as well as physical.

She nodded, unsure as to whether she should even speak. "A quiet spirit," he continued, "is more powerful than a busy, noisy spirit that wastes its energy. This noisy spirit we call 'monkey mind' skitters and chatters and accomplishes nothing.

"Training a spirit to be quiet is simple yet

difficult," Master Lau went on. "Do you understand how something can be opposites at once?"

"I'm not sure," Cassidy said. "I mean, it doesn't sound exactly logical — "

"This is how we train your spirit to be quiet," the *shifu* interrupted. "I will ask you to stand perfectly still, perfectly quiet for an hour. That's all."

"That's simple," Cassidy said. *This is my training? I stand still and do nothing for a whole hour?*

"A simple task, yes. Yet you will see how difficult it is to accomplish." Master Lau turned and began walking away from her. "I'll be in my office for the next hour."

Okay, this should be easy, Cassidy told herself. *I don't understand the purpose, but Master Lau knows what he's doing. If he thinks I should do it, then I should do it.*

She heard the steady tick of a clock somewhere behind her. *I wonder how long it's been so far. Has a minute passed? No, longer than a minute. I've been here, what? Ten minutes at least? No, I've just started, I'm sure ten minutes haven't passed.*

Cassidy stared straight ahead at a blank, cream-colored wall. *Did Master Lau tell me I could look around or not? I don't remember. I think the clock might be on the wall next to his office, but I don't think I'm supposed to turn around. I wonder how long it's been.*

In her mind, Cassidy went over the kicking drills she had been doing on the abandoned playground. *Shouldn't I be training or something? I don't really like this. It's boring, and shouldn't I be learning a new fighting technique, maybe an animal stance? How is this supposed to help?*

Cassidy felt an anxiousness inside, an itchiness to *do* something. *Calm down,* she ordered herself, *just calm down. Maybe if I close my eyes . . .*

Even with her eyes closed, her mind continued to race. Then she took a deep breath and commanded herself to stop. *Just stop thinking! You're not going to make time speed up with all this thinking! Just stop and be still!*

Cassidy willed herself to be calm, and gradually she felt herself enter a quiet state where the thoughts stopped whirling. And when she did, she saw an image begin to form: the two women from her dream, standing beside a clear pool. The picture in her mind was so beautiful and restful that she dared not move a muscle and cause it to disappear.

Ng Mui spoke. *"Your mind should be as calm as this pool. Your thoughts are like random stones that disturb the calm pool and fill it with useless ripples that go on and on. Throw no stones into the pool, Mingmei, and you will achieve the calm mind of a warrior."*

Cassidy visualized the calm pool. She stood perfectly quiet and perfectly still and followed the instructions from her ancestors. She threw no stones into the still, blue water.

Finally Cassidy heard the door to Master Lau's office open and his almost-silent footsteps as he crossed the floor. She waited until he stood in front of her and then opened her eyes.

She tried to read Master Lau's face, but as usual, he offered no expression that gave away his feelings. He didn't ask her if the task had been difficult or easy. In fact, he didn't ask her anything at all. He seemed to be studying her. She wondered if he realized how much she was changing. *Of course he knows that I'm changing. He's my teacher.*

ᔆᔆᔆᔆᔆ

"I had my first private lesson with Master Lau today," Cassidy told James on the phone that night.

"Yeah?" James said. "So does he have you jumping swords or pole fighting?"

"Neither," Cassidy said, fiddling with the plate of peanut butter crackers sitting in front of her. "I stood still for an hour—an entire hour doing nothing."

"Sounds like my kind of training," James told her with a laugh.

"Has he called your dad about the private lessons yet?" she asked.

"No. At least I don't think so. And Majesta hasn't said anything about it, either. In fact, she's asked me if we could train together some."

Majesta again! Cassidy's jaw clenched. *They talk all the time! And now they're going to train together, too?*

"Well, anyway, I'm really glad you're going, James," Cassidy said, hoping he couldn't hear the anger she felt. "I think it'll be a good trip. Maybe we can do other stuff when we're there—not just the tournament, you know?"

"Yeah, I saw the schedule. There's free time built in. It'll just be kind of weird to go back. Weird and—" James stopped, and Cassidy knew that he meant to say *sad*, that it would be sad to go back.

"Anyway," he continued, "I haven't found much on the other two coins. My dad's got a ton of stuff, and it just takes time to go through it all. There's a great library in Hong Kong, though, and all that kind of information's indexed, so it'll be a lot easier to find what we're looking for."

"That's months away, though," Cassidy said. "I've been looking at the fourth coin—and it kind of spooks me."

"The fourth one is the coin with the woman on it, right?"

"Yeah, a woman holding a sword," Cassidy said. "She's holding the sword in front of her face. Well, in front of *half* of her face."

"Blade pointed up or down?"

"Up, why? Does that mean something?"

"It's a symbol of power or victory if it's pointed up and a symbol of defeat if it's pointed down."

"Okay, so I guess that could be good if it means *my* victory. But what about the woman, James? What's she supposed to represent?"

"Well, a woman with a sword just kind of represents the female *warrior*—but that could mean—

actually, I really don't know what it means as far as *demons* are concerned."

Cassidy's eyes narrowed as she thought about the coin and the reflections she'd been seeing. She was about to try and explain it to James—despite how far-fetched a reflection with a mind of its own might sound—when his call waiting clicked. "Hold on," he said. "Call coming in."

While Cassidy waited, she wondered if she could suggest going out to his house again. It made sense: that's where all his dad's books were, and together they could look for information about the coins. *We'd take the ferry together, like before, and then his dad could drive me back. Or maybe James could drive me home this time . . .* She popped one of the crackers into her mouth.

"Hey, Cass, gotta go," James said, coming back on the line. "Majesta's on her way over. I'll call you later. And don't worry, we'll figure this out."

Cassidy seethed as she took a swig of milk and swallowed hard. *Majesta's on her way over so she and James can train together? Why does she even have to go with us? The trip would be so much better if she stayed home.*

"What did you say?" James asked.

She cleared her throat. "What? I didn't say anything," Cassidy told him. She swallowed again, her anger like a hot stone at the back of her throat.

"It sounded like you just said that the trip would be better if Majesta stayed home."

Chapter Twenty-Five

James heard that? Cassidy had thought it, but she knew that she hadn't said it out loud.

"No," Cassidy said quickly. "I said that . . . that Majesta's probably really glad that . . . you're not staying home, that you're going with us."

There was silence on the other end, and then James finally spoke. "Come on, Cass, it sounded like you said . . . Okay, forget it, whatever."

"I didn't say it, okay?" Cassidy told him. "I don't know what you heard. Maybe it's a bad connection or something."

"Sure, a bad connection, right."

"I'll see you Wednesday at Wing Chun," Cassidy said, eager to get off the phone before James heard something else that she didn't say.

As Cassidy hung up the phone, her face burning in embarrassment, she saw her reflection in the pane of her window. The girl who looked exactly like Cassidy hung up the phone at the exact same time. But then she turned toward Cassidy, put her hand up to her cheek, and mouthed the word, *Oops.*

Cassidy lost control. She ran to the window, smacked the frame, and hollered, *"Who are you?!"* But the girl didn't respond. The image wavered and then it was gone, leaving behind only Cassidy's reflection—looking angry, frightened, and totally confused.

☙☙☙☙☙

Cassidy waited outside for Eliza to finish cheerleading practice. Eliza had avoided her ever since the . . . *exorcism* . . . but Cassidy hoped she'd be ready to talk by now. She really wanted to make things right with her friend, and she only had a few minutes before she had to get to her private lesson with Master Lau.

Eliza burst out the gym doors, surrounded by some of the other cheerleaders. The girls were laughing, and Cassidy smiled, happy—and relieved—to hear Eliza's real laugh instead of that demonic, crazy one.

"Hey, Eliza," Cassidy called.

Eliza's head whipped around at the sound of

Cassidy's voice. She frowned. "Hey, Cass."

"So, Cass, Eliza told us about the trip to Hong Kong," Tamika said. "Congratulations, girl!"

The other cheerleaders asked for details, when she'd be going, how long she'd be there, how many kids would be competing in the tournament. But Eliza hung back, never saying a word.

"So who else is going?" Tamika asked.

"Um, Luis Alvarez, James Tang—"

"James Tang," one of the cheerleaders, Tyra, interrupted. "Remember, Tamika, he was at your Halloween party? Dressed as a killer Zorro?"

"Oh my God, yeah, I totally remember Zorro," Tamika said. "What a hottie!"

"Yeah," Tyra said, "and isn't he dating that cheerleader from Wilder? Majesta something?"

Is James actually dating Majesta? Cassidy thought. *Like, DATING, dating her?*

"I need to get out of here," Tyra said, and pulled something from her backpack. "I'm meeting my dad in, like, ten minutes, and he has zero patience."

"Cool iPod," Cassidy said, noticing the sleek black MP3 player in Tyra's hand. She quickly glanced over at Eliza, hoping that maybe she would join in on the conversation.

"I just got it a couple of days ago, for my birthday." Tyra handed the small device to Cassidy. "It weighs, like, *nothing* at all. And it holds a boatload of songs—this one's got four gigs."

"It's so tiny," Cassidy said. "I'd love to have one for when I run."

"Yeah, it's great for that." Tyra pulled a thin nylon case out of her backpack—black with white polka dots all over it. "I just got this skin—but it's an armband, too. Really great for running."

"It's totally cool," Cassidy said, handing the iPod back to Tyra. "Maybe someday . . ." But she doubted an iPod was anywhere in her near future.

"Uh, we have to get going," Eliza said.

"I thought maybe we —" Cassidy began, but the cold look on Eliza's face told her there was no point in finishing. "Uh, so see you around," she said.

It was clear Eliza didn't want to be her friend anymore. And the worst part was—Cassidy didn't blame her.

❧ ❧ ❧ ❧ ❧

"In *chi sau*, sticking hands practice, you have become very adept at anticipating your opponent's next move," said Master Lau to Cassidy at her private session later that afternoon. He crossed the gym and headed toward Cassidy, holding a small black sash and a bamboo pole. "You've developed a sensitivity to your opponents. You've begun to pick up on the tiniest cues—the flutter of an eyelash, the twitch of a muscle, the feather touch of a wrist too close."

So would this be more sticking hands? Cassidy

wondered. She hoped so. The sensitivity that Master Lau was talking about had been very helpful in her battles with the three demons—watching, waiting for just the right moment to strike.

"Follow me," Master Lau said, and led to her to the center of the gym, where a red circle about three feet in diameter had been drawn on the wood floor. Cassidy stood where Master Lau indicated.

"You will defend yourself from that spot," he said. "You may not step out of the circle."

And then he began to walk around the circle, tapping it with the end of the bamboo pole at various points. Cassidy watched him, unsure of what he was asking her to do. "Just listen," he said.

The bamboo was hollow and made sharp clacks when he tapped the pole hard on the floor. But some taps were light and made no more than a slight brushing sound. Then Master Lau surprised Cassidy by bringing the tip of the bamboo pole up and lunging forward. Instinctively she deflected the strike. *So this is the exercise. I can't move out of the circle, and I've got to watch Master Lau and anticipate where he's going to strike with the bamboo.*

"Now, please, Cassidy," Master Lau said, handing her the black sash he'd brought out with him. "Cover your eyes with this and tie it securely. Make sure no light gets in."

I'm going to be blindfolded! How am I supposed to fight if I can't SEE my opponent? But Cassidy trusted Master

Lau and did as she was told.

With the blindfold in place, Cassidy's world went dark and seemed to close in around her. She wondered how she was supposed to stay within the circle if she couldn't see.

"We will start slow, Cassidy," Master Lau said, and she could tell from his voice that he'd moved to her right. She turned to her right without moving from the circle. *Calm your mind,* she told herself, remembering to use the lesson from the week before. *Throw no stones in the pool. A quiet spirit is more sensitive than a busy one.*

She heard the bamboo tap the floor, and she raised her arm to shield herself. Next she heard three taps in a row, but she somehow *sensed* that those taps wouldn't be followed by an attack. A small brushing tap behind her sent her whirling, jutting her palm out just as the rounded end of the pole made contact.

Again and again Master Lau tapped the floor and lunged forward. Cassidy deflected each strike, sensing where he was even before he brought the bamboo pole down on the floor. *It's so weird,* she thought. *I can hear him—his feet on the floor, the slight swish of cloth as he moves, even a small whistling sound of air passing through the bamboo. But am I staying within the circle?*

Master Lau tapped the pole and she blocked the strike, realizing then that each tap resulted in a slight but distinctive echo against the walls of the gym. If she moved even six inches out of the circle, the echo would sound different. *My mind must be making the slight adjustments, just inches one way or another, to keep me within the circle.*

Cassidy stood ready to meet Master Lau's next move, but she sensed a hesitation and then she heard him take a step back. "You may remove the blindfold," he said.

She reached up and pulled off the blindfold. The bright fluorescent light burned her eyes for a moment. Master Lau stood in front of her, holding the bamboo pole at his side. "You did very well, Cassidy," he said to her, his voice betraying a hint of surprise. "You possess a keen sensitivity to sound."

"Thank you, *Shifu*," she said.

Master Lau turned and began walking back to his office.

That was kind of abrupt, she thought. They usually bowed to each other before ending class. *He's probably got another student coming in,* she decided with a shrug. She looked down and saw that she was still standing in the exact center of the red circle.

❧❧❧❧❧

When Cassidy left the studio and started toward the bus stop, she was still feeling energized by the drill. *Master Lau said I had a keen sensitivity to sound, but it was more than that. It felt like I knew where he was going to be even before he got there.* She replayed the drill in her mind. Her *still and quiet* mind. *That's it, too,* she realized.

When my mind is still and quiet, I can do more—I can feel more.

Cassidy decided to get off the bus two stops early and walk the rest of the way home. She wandered down a small path toward the lake shore. It was still early enough that people were out walking. The air was crisp, and the water was as blue as the sky.

She continued down the path, making a small turn that led to a little clearing with a few benches and a stone picnic table. This part of the lake was a haven for all types of wildlife. The water was shallow here, dotted with a series of large stones that jutted up from the surface. The boulders provided the birds with a perfect perch on which to rest and to dive at the fish.

Cassidy's breath caught. A crane stood at the water's edge, poised and perfectly still. She remembered the day Master Lau taught them to do the crane stance. The lesson was about developing balance. It had been difficult, but Cassidy had mastered it quickly, something inside her responding to the image of the beautiful birds she'd seen so often on the lake.

She stepped closer to the water's edge to get a better look at the bird. Its white feathers glistened and caught the golden light of the sun that hung low in the western sky. It looked once toward Cassidy and then lifted up, flying out over the water before settling again farther down the shore.

Cassidy followed the flight of the bird with her eyes, wishing that she could move like that. She bent her left leg as if practicing—and then she began rising from where she stood, her right leg outstretched in an impossible leap toward a large gray boulder *at least ten feet away!* She landed gracefully and looked back at where she'd just come from. *How did that happen? I practically flew here! No, that's impossible.*

She eyed another large stone jutting out of the lake at least fifteen feet away. *Could I do it again?*

She glanced toward the crane. It stood with its head tilted to the side, watching her curiously. Cassidy took a deep breath and leaped out and up. She found herself moving through the air, across the water, in long, easy strides. There was no mistaking it this time. She was flying. Just like in the martial arts movies.

Cassidy landed softly and soundlessly on the flat surface of a boulder more than twenty feet from the shore. An overwhelming feeling of pure joy bubbled inside her, making her feel lighter than air.

The crane, close enough now for Cassidy to touch, lifted up one last time and flew into the sunset. She watched it disappear into the pinkish golden light.

Cassidy looked back toward the distant shoreline and smiled. She was tempted to simply keep going—to hold on to the exhilaration that electrified every cell of her body. But Cassidy knew it was time to go back. She emptied her mind of every stray thought and then stepped out, running through the crisp winter chill, her feet never touching the frigid water. It was the most wonderful sensation she had ever experienced.

❧ Chapter Twenty-Six

Mr. Edwards wore a serious and pained look as he gazed out over the hundreds of students gathered for the Tuesday morning assembly. "Such a disappointment," he said. "But I'm sure that whoever took this person's property will do the right thing and return it."

"What's he talking about?" Cassidy asked Tamika. Normally Cassidy would have asked Eliza. Normally Eliza would have been right by Cassidy's side. But now Eliza was seated clear across the gym floor next to Tyra, as far away from Cassidy as could be. Cassidy had been thinking about her evening at the lake — remembering how light she'd felt as she ran over the water — such a contrast to the heavy feeling she had now as she sat in the gym listening to Mr. Edwards. "He said somebody stole something, right?"

"An iPod, and it was Tyra's," Tamika said. "Disappeared from her gym bag yesterday."

"You know who you are, and you know what you've done," Mr. Edwards continued. "The property may be returned to the office *anonymously* — no questions asked."

∂∂∂∂∂

Cassidy took her Spanish book from the top shelf of her locker and reached toward the back, where her second-period notebook had fallen behind a stack of other books.

"Hey, Cass," Tamika said, coming up behind her. "Need help?" Cassidy was straining to reach behind the stack but couldn't quite get to the spiral edge of the notebook, which seemed to be caught on something.

"Yeah, thanks, Tamika — it's my notebook. I think it's stuck." Cassidy stood aside while the taller Tamika reached over the jumbled stack of books to the back.

"Got it," Tamika said, pulling out the notebook.

Her eyes widened as she saw the headphone wires that were caught in the spiral spine of Cassidy's notebook — wires that were plugged into an iPod encased in a distinctive black-and-white polka-dot skin.

"This is Tyra's," Tamika said. "Cassidy, this is Tyra's! What are you doing with it? Did you steal it?"

"No!" Cassidy said, alarmed that Tamika could even think such a thing. "Of course I didn't take it!" Her mind raced frantically as she tried to come up with some sort of explanation.

"But this is definitely Tyra's iPod. It's her case and everythi—"

"I—I found it," she stammered lamely. "I was going to return it as soon as I saw her, but then I got all caught up in other stuff and . . ." Her voice trailed off. Cassidy had a sick feeling deep in her stomach. She was pretty sure Tamika wasn't buying her explanation.

Tamika just stood there holding the iPod in her hand, staring at Cassidy.

"Tamika, I would never steal anything. Come on, you *know* me! This is crazy!"

"I guess . . ." She wrapped the cord around the little device. "But I think I'll just give this to Tyra myself."

"Sure, of course. I mean, you'll probably run into her before I will."

Tamika gave a halfhearted nod.

"So, uh, say hi to Tyra for me," Cassidy said.

"Whatever." Tamika turned and disappeared down the hall.

Cassidy's hand shook as she shut her locker. She was no good at lying. And she had no idea how that iPod *had* ended up in her locker.

Just like I have no idea how those jeans got charged on my mom's card and then ended up under my bed. If only I could get to the bottom of this.

Cassidy strolled to the water fountain and held down the button, taking deep swallows of cold water, willing herself to calm down. But her mind raced, the unanswered questions whirling.

She lifted her head and saw her reflection in the glass wall that enclosed the administrative office. She stared at the image of a dark-haired girl with glittering, laughing eyes and a mouth stretched wide in amusement. *That is not me!* Cassidy thought, her heart pounding, the hot feeling of tears burning her eyes. *So why does she look like my identical twin?*

Chapter Twenty-Seven

The bus to downtown Seattle seemed to hit every green light for once, and Cassidy arrived on South King Street in record time. She glanced at her watch and realized that she had more than enough time to stop in Ethos Café and work on her geometry homework before Wing Chun class.

She also knew that James often stopped in at Ethos and hoped that she might run into him. After all, James might have some information on the fourth coin, and she wanted to tell him about the stolen iPod *and* about the terrible reflections she had been seeing. Maybe she should also mention their phone conversation and the comment James thought she'd made about Majesta.

And then it occurred to her—maybe the comment was related to the *weird reflections*. Maybe all the strange things that were happening had something to do with that reflection.

The door to the café squeaked as Cassidy pushed it open, and she heard Majesta's laugh even before she saw her. Majesta and James sat together at a small table near the back. Their chairs were pushed close together, and as Cassidy watched, Majesta reached out to brush away a thin line of cappuccino foam from James's upper lip.

They both looked toward the door when Cassidy entered. James raised his hand in a wave—still laughing as Majesta continued to pat his mouth with her napkin. Cassidy walked straight up to the counter and grabbed a bottled water from the case next to the cashier. She dropped her money on the counter and left, James's and Majesta's laughter still ringing in her ears as the door closed behind her.

What was so funny? she wondered. *Majesta is acting so . . . so stupid! Is James actually falling for that ridiculous giggling? It's so obvious. And embarrassing. That's what it is—she's just embarrassing herself, the way she's throwing herself at him!*

Cassidy sat on the steps outside Master Lau's and unscrewed her water bottle. Her face felt hot, and the cool water felt good as it went down her throat.

With her geometry book open and pencil poised over her notebook, Cassidy tried to concentrate on her homework, but it was impossible. A slight breeze riffled her paper, and she couldn't hold it in place and balance her book on her knees at the same time. *I should just go back in there,* she thought. *It's a free country. I should march in there, sit at a table, and do my homework*—but even as she thought it, she knew there was no way she could walk back into the café and face James and Majesta, looking so much like—well, like they were in love with each other.

Cassidy snapped her textbook closed and shoved it deep inside her backpack, giving up on getting any homework done before Wing Chun. *Why did Master Lau choose Majesta in the first place? She's not even that good! And how am I supposed to talk to James about the fourth coin if he's with her all the time?*

During class Cassidy tried to block them out, but Master Lau paired James and Majesta for drills, and Cassidy couldn't stop herself from looking at them every chance she got. *If I have to spend two weeks in Hong Kong watching those two flirt with each other, I'd rather stay home!* she thought. *No!* she decided. *Majesta should be the one staying home. She cares more about being a cheerleader and looking good. She doesn't really care about Wing Chun or the competition . . .*

Class was almost over when Cassidy was paired with Luis for *chi sau*. She figured it'd be no contest. After all, she'd excelled at the bamboo pole exercise with Master Lau and she'd been blindfolded!

But her anger distracted her, and Luis was able to deflect most of her strikes. For the first time since she had received the coins, she was actually letting her emotions get in the way of her performance. And it was all because there was no more denying the fact that James had feelings for Majesta. It was as plain as daylight.

"What's up with you, Cass?" Luis asked. "You just doing this to make me look good?"

"Shut up, Luis," Cassidy said. "I'm just off today, okay?"

"Come on, you're Master Lau's favorite—you can't let him down," Luis teased, moving slowly to the right, then quickly to the left and catching Cassidy totally off guard.

"I'm not his favorite," Cassidy countered.

"Well, you're the only one he's called in for private lessons," Luis said. "I haven't been called. Neither has James or Majesta."

Cassidy was too upset to care what a huge compliment Master Lau was paying her by calling her in for their private sessions. "Majesta shouldn't even be going with us," Cassidy said sharply. "Look at her—she's pathetic!" Cassidy glanced over at Majesta, paired with James. She was leaning in close to him, her eyes locked with his.

"Are you jealous?" Luis asked. "Because of James?"

"I am *not* jealous," Cassidy snapped. "Why should I be jealous of Majesta? It's sad, really, the way she acts around him."

"Right." Luis didn't sound convinced.

"All I'm saying is that she's not that good. I don't think it would be such a great loss if Majesta wasn't on the team. I'm sure Master Lau could find somebody better to take her place."

"Sure, Cass, whatever," Luis said, and then lunged forward, taking her left arm in a grab that Cassidy never saw coming.

അ അ അ അ അ

After class was over, Cassidy took her time changing, staying far back in the corner of the dressing room until it was empty. She walked through the silent gymnasium, hoping that she'd wasted enough time so that she wouldn't have to run into James and Majesta out on the sidewalk. She'd seen enough of both of them for one day. *I guess I can forget about talking to James at the moment,* she realized.

As she pushed open the studio door, she saw Majesta sitting on the bottom step. Majesta's older sister was speaking on her cell phone and lightly touching Majesta's wrist, which was swollen and purple. There was also a nasty red scrape on the side of her face.

Luis squatted on the bottom step next to

Majesta. He looked up at Cassidy when she opened the door.

"What happened?" Cassidy asked.

It was Majesta who answered, her voice bitter. "What happened? You knocked me down the steps— *that's* what happened! And then you just went back inside, like a coward!"

"But I didn't!" Cassidy said, shocked that somebody would even think she would do such a thing.

"Cassidy, I saw you," Luis said, standing. "You opened the door, and Majesta was standing right there on the top step. You pushed her. I *saw* you push her! And then you went back inside like nothing happened!"

Chapter Twenty-Eight

Majesta and her sister walked to the car, and Luis followed them with Majesta's backpack. He held the door for her as she slid inside. "You think it's broken?" Luis asked.

"Hopefully just a sprain," Majesta's sister said. "Mom's meeting us at the emergency room to get it X-rayed."

"I'll check on you later, Majesta," Luis said just before closing the door.

Cassidy hadn't moved from where she stood on the top step. She felt paralyzed by the realization that Luis truly believed she was responsible for

Majesta's fall.

Luis looked toward the uptown bus that had just pulled up to the corner in a hiss of brakes. He grabbed his bag from the bottom step and ran toward the waiting bus, not even looking toward Cassidy. She sprinted after him, following him up the steps and down the narrow aisle of the bus, where he found a seat near the back.

Cassidy scooted in next to him even though it was clear that he wasn't making room for her on the seat. "Luis, I didn't do it. You have to believe me!" she said, her voice very close to breaking. "Please, Luis, you *know* me! I would never hurt anyone!"

"I know what I saw," Luis said, his face turned toward the window.

She could see his reflection as he stared out into the darkness beyond the window. And next to Luis's frowning reflection, Cassidy, once again, saw her own reflection—laughing, positively giddy at the evil thing she'd just done. She had a furious urge to hurl herself at the laughing girl in the window and pummel her.

Suppressing a shudder, Cassidy glanced at Luis. She guessed that he didn't or *couldn't* see the awful reflection in the glass. He sat in stony silence looking out the window at the blurred streetlights of Seattle. She considered for a moment telling Luis everything, but she knew there was no way she could explain it without sounding like she was making up a ridiculous story—a story that would sound like an excuse for doing something horrible. *Luis would never believe me—not in a million years.*

At the next stop a woman got off, leaving an empty seat, and Cassidy stood up to take it. Her legs felt weak as she made her way up the aisle. Luis wanted nothing to do with her, and she couldn't blame him. She had to figure this out and make it stop before somebody else got hurt—and she lost all of her friends, and her parents stopped trusting her, and who knew what else.

James. She had to talk to James. If he was really her ally, he would help her get to the bottom of all the weirdness. And if he wasn't her ally, then now was as good a time as any to find out. She needed to tell him about the reflections, about the iPod, and—worst of all—she'd have to tell him about Majesta's accident. He hadn't been out on the sidewalk, so he must have left before it happened. Would he believe her? He *had* to believe her. He had to help her find a way to stop whatever was going on.

But what if he couldn't? *Maybe I should go to Master Lau.* She shook her head at the thought. *How could I tell Master Lau? I'd have to tell him about the stolen iPod, about being jealous of Majesta.* No, she realized, there was no way on earth that she could talk to Master Lau about this. He might change his mind about Hong Kong—he might decide she wasn't even worthy of going!

And there was something else, too, that bothered Cassidy about telling Master Lau. She probably couldn't tell him just part of it this time, the way she had when Eliza had been cursed by the fox demon. She wasn't convinced he had really believed her explanation—and there would be even more questions this time. She might have to tell him *all* of it—the coins, the winged snake, the plague ghost, the fox demon—*all of it*. And she just couldn't do that. It could influence his opinion of her. He could begin to regard her as trouble or a security risk, and then he might rethink his decision to bring her to Hong Kong. And at the moment, Hong Kong seemed like the only really good thing in Cassidy's life.

෨෨෨෨෨

"Luis said he actually *saw* you push her?" James asked.

Cassidy had made herself call James as soon as she got home. And she'd gotten the hard part over with first, telling James about Majesta's fall.

"Yeah, he did," Cassidy said. "And Majesta, too. I'm pretty sure she hates me right now."

Cassidy could hear James breathing on the other end of the phone. *He probably thinks I pushed her, too. He remembers what I said about wishing she would stay home. He didn't believe me when I told him it was a bad connection.*

"There's something else," she said. "I don't know if any of these things are connected, but I'm starting to think that maybe they are." She told him about the stolen iPod in her locker and the strange reflections she'd seen. She reminded him about the jeans charged on her mother's card and then finding them later in her room—that she'd even seen the reflection wearing them. As she talked, she realized how it must sound to him. "James, I know it probably sounds like I really did all this stuff, but I didn't!"

"Okay, let's think about this. You wanted the jeans. You were mad at your mom because she wouldn't get them for you, and then they're charged on her card, right?"

"Yeah, and then later I find them in my room," Cassidy said, cringing at the facts.

"So then," James continued, "you tell Tyra you want an iPod like hers and it ends up in your locker."

"Right," Cassidy said. "You should have seen Tamika's face—she *really* didn't believe me." Cassidy felt sick. Her life was spinning totally out of control.

"Okay, so it's, like, whenever you want something or you get mad or whatever, this evil twin appears and does the dirty work for you, right?"

"Uh, yeah, I guess," Cassidy said, but she was thinking, *An evil twin? That's ridiculous.* "I mean, I guess that's what it *seems* like."

"So, why were you mad at Majesta?" James asked. "Or what did she have that you wanted? Why would the *evil twin,* or whatever it is, push Majesta down the stairs?"

Cassidy swallowed hard. She didn't want to answer this. What could she say — *You, James, she has you! That's why I was mad at Majesta—that's why I've been wishing that she wouldn't go to Hong Kong with us!*

"We have kind of a history," Cassidy told him, hoping it sounded convincing. "There's always been a little . . . competition or something."

She stopped, wondering if that was enough, but James didn't say anything.

"That's not the point, anyway," she continued. "The point is that *somebody* or *something* is doing these awful things. Both Luis and Majesta saw a girl they *thought* was me — but it wasn't!"

And then James said something that Cassidy wasn't sure she heard correctly. "But what if it *was* you, Cassidy?"

Chapter Twenty-Nine

"What!" Cassidy said, stunned. Did James really believe she would lie to her mother, steal from her friends, push Majesta down the stairs? "James, have you even been listening to me?"

"Hold on," James said. "I didn't mean *you* exactly. There's a myth I read in one of my dad's books. It's about a fighter who has to defeat his *dark half* before becoming a warrior."

"His *dark half*?" Cassidy asked. She picked up the little jade dog charm on her nightstand and rubbed it as she listened to James.

"Yeah, like his dark thoughts and emotions—

anger, greed, doubt, you know, all the negative stuff inside. Anyway, in the story he goes into the mountains and confronts this dark side of himself. It's like, to become a true warrior, he has to face the darkness inside himself and defeat it before he can face the darkness of the world."

"So you *do* think this could be connected to the coin," Cassidy said. "All the bad stuff that's been happening . . ."

"Yeah, maybe. Does that seem so bizarre?"

"A little. I mean, all the other demons were . . . well, demons. You're talking about . . ." Cassidy realized then that James was actually saying that *she* was the demon in this case—or at least the negative qualities inside her. *Could that be true?* she wondered. *Am I angry, greedy, jealous? Yeah, sometimes. But isn't everybody?*

"I read this really cool quote that makes tons of sense," James said. *"It's easier to face the darkness in others than the darkness within ourselves."*

"Yeah, it's cool, all right, but what does it mean, exactly?"

"Think about it, Cass," James said. "We don't like to even *admit* that we have dark thoughts. It's always easier to see bad stuff in other people than to see it in ourselves. The only way to *defeat* something—no matter what it is—is to admit that it's there. To really *face* it."

She pictured the engraving on the fourth coin—the woman holding an upright sword, half the woman's face covered. *The dark half, maybe? Could the sword symbolize the warrior's victory over her own dark half?*

"So, the demon I have to face this time is *me*?" Cassidy said.

"I don't know if that's the demon or not—but think about it, Cass. It's like with each battle, you're getting stronger—but you're not there yet, right? So this time you have to face—well, maybe you have to face *yourself*."

Downstairs, Cassidy's mother was calling her to dinner. *How long have I been on the phone with James?*

"I need to go, James," Cassidy said. "My mom's calling me. And this is . . . this is a lot to think about."

"It's gonna be okay, Cass," James told her, his voice so velvety smooth that Cassidy could almost feel it against her skin. "I know it's a lot, but you can do this. I know you can."

"You really think so?" Cassidy asked, wishing she didn't have to get off the phone.

"Tell you what," James said, "let's meet tomorrow after school and we'll talk about it some more, okay?"

"Okay," Cassidy said. "You wanna just come by the house? Maybe we can walk down to the lake if the weather's nice."

"Sounds good. I'll see you then," James said.

The next afternoon Cassidy looked out her window and saw James walking up the driveway toward her front door. He wore a dark green sweatshirt with a pale yellow logo on the front and a faded pair of jeans, ripped at one knee. She loved to watch him walk—hands in pockets, head tilted down, shoulders hunched slightly forward. *And he's coming to see me!*

Her heart leaped in her chest as the doorbell rang. And then she remembered why he was there. *Why do we have to talk about demons, coins, evil twins? Why can't we talk about music or movies or just about anything else besides this crazy stuff that's happening in my life!*

"Hey, James," Cassidy said, opening the door and stepping out onto the front stoop with him. "You wanna walk down to the lake?"

"Sure," he said. "It's, like, almost spring today."

"Yeah, it's weird, huh?" Cassidy said. "And this is just March. It should be cold out here."

Cassidy matched her stride to his as they strolled down the path that led toward the clearing at the lake's edge. "So . . . did you talk to Majesta?" Cassidy asked, almost hoping that he hadn't. "Is she okay?"

"Yeah," James said. "It's just a slight sprain. She'll be fine. But you're right—she's pretty upset with you. And totally convinced that you pushed her."

Cassidy had half hoped that maybe Majesta would think about it and realize that it *hadn't* been

Cassidy after all. But that was obviously wishful thinking. Like wishing that Eliza would be her friend again. Or that life could be normal.

"So what am I going to do?" Cassidy asked. "I don't want anybody else to get hurt. I have to *do* something!" She kicked a rock and sent it spinning along the road. "But *what*?"

"I think," James said, "that you're going to have to draw out your evil twin, so you can face her."

They had just reached a secluded area of the lakefront, sheltered by a long row of evergreens. It was the same place where Cassidy had seen her ancestors the morning she had been out running.

"Listen, I need to tell you something," James said, settling onto a bench.

Cassidy sat beside him, a prickly feeling racing along her spine. James was fixing her with a strange, intense gaze. His dark eyes seemed to bore straight into her.

"What is it?" Cassidy asked, her heart beating a little faster.

"I changed my mind about Hong Kong. I'm not going."

Cassidy stared at him in disbelief. "But you said—"

He interrupted her. "Look, I know how you feel about *the team* and all, but I just don't want to go."

"I can't believe this!" Cassidy said, her voice rising. "We're all counting on you." *He promised! Why would he change his mind now?*

James shrugged. "I've already talked to Majesta about it, and she understands. I know you don't really like her, Cass, but if you got to know her better . . ."

He wants me to get to know Majesta better! Is he out of his mind? The image of James and Majesta in the café together scrolled across the screen in Cassidy's head. All the anger and bitterness she had felt that day spiked inside her, and she wanted to scream.

"Look, James," Cassidy said, breathing hard now. "I don't know what you—" And then she stopped.

There was something about his expression, the way his eyes studied her. It hit her—*He's doing this on purpose! He's trying to make me angry, to draw out the evil twin!*

James quickly looked away, then back at her. "What makes you think Lau is so great, anyway?" he sneered. "I swear, you've got him up on a pedestal, like one of the Chinese Immortals. He's just a kung fu teacher, as flawed as anyone else."

"Stop changing the subject," Cassidy snapped. "What's the real reason you don't want to go to Hong Kong? Not that it's any of my business—we're just a *team*, after all." She intentionally filled her words with sarcasm and anger, wondering if their act was working.

James shrugged. "I'm really pretty sick of it— actually, bored to death. And I can stay here and be bored. I don't need to go halfway around the world."

"Oh, you're *bored*," Cassidy said. "Have you told Master Lau yet? Do you realize he's *counting* on you—like we all are?"

"Yeah, Lau's counting on me to win so that he looks like some hotshot *master*. I don't want to be a part of it. Besides, I've got my life here in Seattle now. I lived in Hong Kong, remember? I really don't need to go back."

Cassidy was stunned. That last bit didn't sound like an act at all. Those bitter words sounded as if they were coming from James's heart—even if he wasn't being completely honest about *why* he didn't want to go back.

"I can't believe you," she said, surprised by the force of her own words. "You're being totally selfish! And I don't understand why you say those things about Master Lau. You act like you know more than he does, like he has *nothing* to teach you. But you're wrong!" Cassidy was practically screaming at him now. "You don't know *half* of what Master Lau knows. With your attitude, you're lucky he even lets you *stay* in the class!"

Cassidy jumped to her feet. Now she *was* truly angry. *It's time to stop this game before it gets any more real,* she thought. Her pulse raced, and her face felt hot.

"Look, James, do whatever you want, okay? I really don't care. The team will do just fine without you—maybe even better." She stalked away from him, leaving him sitting on the bench as she started up the trail that led out of the park.

When she reached the thick patch of trees, she heard the crunch of dried leaves. Cassidy turned and watched as someone stepped off the trail and made her way over to the bench where James sat alone.

The fine hairs on the back of Cassidy's neck stood straight up. *My twin!* The girl was her exact double, dressed in the same jeans and gray wool sweater with the same orange stripes down the sleeves.

Cassidy hid behind a large spruce tree. *This is too bizarre!* She peered around the trunk, staring at her double, the one who stole, the one who'd pushed Majesta. *What did James say—she's you, all your dark, negative thoughts?*

Cassidy felt sick as she saw the girl sit down beside James. *Does he know it's the double? How could he?* she realized with a pang. *She looks exactly like me!*

"James, look, I'm sorry, okay?" the double said. Even her voice was a pitch-perfect match for Cassidy's. "I shouldn't have said those things. I'm sorry I got so upset!"

She was so perfectly, totally *believable!* Cassidy wanted to run out and confront her right there. But she waited.

Cassidy could tell that James was confused. He stared at the other Cassidy, as if trying to figure out if it was her or not.

"It's just that I *really* like you. The truth is, I

want you to go to Hong Kong so we can be together. And that's why I don't want Majesta to go."

Oh no! Cassidy gave a silent groan, her face flaming with embarrassment. This was not at all what she expected. Her evil twin was supposed to act on her anger, not tell James how she felt about him!

"It makes me sick to see you with Majesta," Cassidy's double continued. "I'm glad she fell down the steps. I just wish it would keep her from going to Hong Kong. *You're* the only reason she wants to go. She doesn't really care about Wing Chun. Besides, she's not really good enough."

Cassidy gripped the tree so hard that the bark bit into the soft flesh of her fingertips. Her embarrassment had turned to bone-deep shame. *All my meanest, most selfish thoughts on display for James.* She wanted to run away, but she felt paralyzed.

James was as silent as the trees around them. His dark eyes seemed to be searching the face of the girl in front of him.

The double reached out and took James by the arm—the *exact* way Cassidy had once seen Majesta take James by the arm—like he was all hers and she wanted everybody to know it.

"I've been crushing on you since the first day I saw you," the girl said, smiling. "I can't stop thinking about you."

Cassidy couldn't watch any longer. She felt a hot pressure behind her eyes, but she was determined not to cry—not yet, anyway—not until she could get home. And that's where she needed to be—home. She ran back up the trail away from the lake, away from the sight of her double confessing her love for James—while he looked . . . what? Surprised—or repulsed?

She knew she could never face him again. But in her haste, her foot slipped on the damp path. She reached out to catch a small bush but missed and found herself sliding downhill and skidding to a stop a short distance from James and the other Cassidy.

Cassidy scrambled to her feet to find her double smiling widely, clearly enjoying Cassidy's humiliation.

Cassidy, more mortified than ever, turned to flee again, but James's voice stopped her.

"You can't run from this," he called. "She's you, Cass, your own dark side. And she's not going away unless you face her and fight."

The double leaned closer to James and wrapped her arm around his even as he began to pull away from her. "Come on, James, is that any way to talk about your new girlfriend?"

Then she turned to Cassidy. "Aren't you happy? We won! We won James away from that nasty Majesta! But maybe next time she's at the top of the steps, you should push a little harder!"

That did it. Cassidy charged at her double, her eyes practically blind from rage and shame. But in the instant before Cassidy reached her, the girl disappeared from James's side and then reappeared standing on a large, flat boulder jutting out of the lake, several feet from the shore. The girl's face — *Cassidy's* face — was reflected a hundred, maybe a *thousand* times in the lake all around her. One moment the reflections looked exactly like Cassidy, and the next they were contorted, laughing, grinning, teasing, taunting her.

"*What's the matter? Jealous? Angry? Scared? Embarrassed? Can't face the truth? I'm your truth, Cassidy!*" The words seemed to echo in her head, but she knew that they weren't just in her head. She knew that James was hearing them, too.

Cassidy stood at the edge of the water. Her many reflections covered the surface of the lake, each one different but equally terrible. Each an ugly, shameful image that claimed to be the real Cassidy.

❧ Chapter Thirty

Cassidy closed her eyes. She couldn't stand to see the monstrous images of herself any longer. She took a deep breath, and as she exhaled, she pictured a clear pool of water. When she opened her eyes, she looked out over the lake and was relieved to see that the reflections in the water were gone. Only the girl — her double, her dark half — remained standing on a boulder near the center of the lake.

"Too bad you can't get to me here, Cassidy," her double teased. "This is where I'll always be. Just out of your reach!"

Cassidy said nothing. She breathed deeply,

using her breath to calm herself while she waited for the perfect moment to strike.

"You can't fight me and you know it!" the double taunted. "After all — I'm *you*!"

Cassidy cringed. She wanted no part of this horrible creature. It made her sick to think that they were alike in any way.

The girl began laughing. "Face it! This is who you are — so just accept it! You've got this terrific crush on James, but you won't tell him — so I did it for you. See — isn't that better? Now he knows!"

Is James still here? Cassidy didn't want to turn around to see if he was behind her. But she had the horrible feeling that he was there — and hearing every humiliating word.

"Same with the jeans. Your mom's such a cheapskate. She won't get you the jeans you want — so I helped you out there, too," the girl said. "But remember, we're the same, Cass — so really *you* got the jeans. Just like *you* took the iPod."

"No!" Cassidy said. "*You* did it! I would never do that to my mother, and I would never steal!"

Now the girl was positively shaking with laughter. "Oh, Cass, get it into your head. You took the card, you charged the jeans, you stole the iPod — and here's the best one — you pushed Majesta Madison down the steps!"

"I didn't!" Cassidy said. "You're lying!"

"Am I? Then tell me, what's the difference

between the two of us?"

Cassidy stared at her twin. She couldn't come up with an answer.

"See, I'm right! We're the same!"

"You're part of me, all right," Cassidy admitted. "The worst of me. But you're not the whole, and you're not what controls me. In fact, you're the part I can fight." To her surprise, her words sounded strong and sure.

Three graceful strides over the water took Cassidy to the first boulder. *I have to do this,* she thought. *This is the only way to make her stop!* She took a quick glance back toward shore and saw that James was standing at the edge of the lake, watching.

Cassidy looked at her twin. She was now standing on an old wooden platform that had once been part of a fishing dock. *Is she running from me?* Cassidy wondered. She studied the face of the girl, who didn't seem to be smirking quite as much as before.

"Let's put on a show for James," her twin said. "Prove to him how powerful you are! He knows you're good. I guess now you want to show him how good!"

"I'm not doing this for James," Cassidy said. "I don't care if he's watching or not. I won't let you control my life!"

Cassidy looked down and saw a silvery handle jutting out of the lake. *What's this?* She reached down and wrapped her fingers around the cool silver hilt of a sword—and then she pulled it out of the water and lifted it high. Cassidy knew nothing about sword fighting, but somehow it felt just right in her hand — the perfect weight, the perfect balance. *I can do this,* Cassidy thought. *I'll use the sword to cut this—this awful thing out of my life!*

She looked across the water at her twin. *That* Cassidy also held a sword. But *her* sword looked as if it were made of bronze, an ancient weapon forged with old magic. Cassidy fought down a shiver of fear.

"Exactly," her twin said, reading her every thought. The girl raised the sword in both hands. She brought it down without much visible force — almost casually — and it sliced through one of the heavy concrete pilings at the edge of the dock, as if the concrete were butter.

Her twin shot Cassidy a wicked smile. "Do you still think you can fight me?"

✿ Chapter Thirty-One

Cassidy, sword in hand, moved out across the lake in large, easy bounds. Her feet touched lightly on one boulder and then another until she landed on the wooden platform where her double stood.

"Majesta really is more beautiful than we are. You know that, don't you?" the double said to her, her sword raised—the mirror image of Cassidy's.

Cassidy didn't speak, but she was forced to take a step back as the double moved closer.

"She's, like, the perfect girl, and trust me, James knows it. In fact, Majesta makes sure that James knows it!"

Cassidy felt a stab of jealousy as the double lunged toward her — the bronze tip pointed straight at her chest. But somehow Cassidy blocked it with her silver blade.

She's going to keep doing this, Cassidy thought. *She'll keep playing on my anger and my jealousy until she gets through my defenses. Until she destroys me.*

I have to clear my mind, Cassidy realized. *No unwanted emotions—no jealousy, no anger.* Keeping her eyes on her twin, Cassidy began to concentrate on the rhythm of her breathing.

Once again her double began to laugh. "Oh, please. Do you really think that will work? Look at James—" She gestured toward the shore. "You want to know what he really thinks about you? He thinks you're a sweet little kid, and sometimes he even feels sorry for you."

The words made Cassidy sick. It was *exactly* what she had feared. James would never see her as anything but a—

The tip of the bronze sword darted past the silver blade, sliced through the sweater, and cut a fine line in Cassidy's forearm. The cut burned, and Cassidy's first instinct was to drop her own sword, but she held on.

Her twin shook her head in mock disappointment. "That's what happens when you let me distract you. I just keep opening up little wounds, finding more ways to get inside and control you."

Cassidy grew icy cold. She would have to defeat—kill—this demon that looked exactly like her, that *was* her.

"You can't do it, can you?" said the double. "I told you—we're the same. Why don't you just give up and accept it?"

I can't look at her, Cassidy realized. *I can't do this if I have to see her.* Cassidy remembered Master Lau's drill with the blindfold. *Pay attention,* she told herself. *Keep a clear mind and just* listen! *You'll know what to do.*

She took a deep breath and closed her eyes.

"Are you still wearing those dorky jeans?" her twin taunted. But Cassidy kept her eyes closed, and when she sensed that the girl's strike was near, she deflected it. She felt the powerful jolt of her silver sword meeting the bronze one and thought that maybe the force of the bronze sword was a little weaker now.

Then Cassidy heard the creak of the boards and realized that her double was moving in behind her. Cassidy spun around, eyes shut but ready.

"You know you'll never be even half as beautiful as Majesta, don't you?" the double said. This time her strike was aimed at Cassidy's legs—but Cassidy jumped at the precise moment she heard the bronze sword cut through the air. Cassidy went on the offensive and slashed at the sword, connected, and heard something change in the way the air moved around the bronze blade. She was almost certain now that she'd at least nicked it, if she didn't cut through it.

Again she wanted to look—but she couldn't. She didn't know what was coming next—what kind of toxic words the girl would throw at her. But Cassidy knew that the only way to fight her was to resist her with everything she had—and to keep cutting away at the awful dark energy with the silver sword.

Where is she now? Cassidy had moved forward aggressively and was fairly sure that she had backed the girl all the way to the edge of the platform. *Yeah, I can hear her—she's right there!*

"Maybe if your mom wasn't so *cheap*, she'd buy you some jeans you look good in," the girl said. "You work for her in that stupid Happy Bunny place and she pays you, like, *nothing*!"

Cassidy's eyes shot open. "That's not true," she said. "My mother is wonderful. She loves me and only wants the best for me!"

Then Cassidy saw them—all across the lake— reflections of familiar faces. Her ancestors. They were with her, sending her their strength and love.

She looked at her twin and spoke the words that she now knew to be the truth. "You don't have power," she declared. She pointed to the faces in the lake. "They do. What matters is my family and friends, and my ancestors and the fight against evil. You may be part of me, but you're the petty part, the part I can push aside. As long as I keep my mind clear and centered, I don't have to make room for you anymore."

This time Cassidy didn't wait for the girl to

strike. She raised the silver sword high above her head and brought it down straight and hard, shattering the bronze blade.

For the first time her twin looked shaken. "You can't do that," she said.

"I just did." Cassidy felt as if her power came from a deep pool within. She felt free—free from anger, from jealousy, and from the negative thoughts that had done nothing but weaken her and make her doubt the power that she had inside. She wasn't surprised when her double wavered, became transparent, and then disappeared in a column of dark mist.

The sword began to feel warm in Cassidy's hands. She looked at the beautiful weapon in amazement as the metal began to soften. The melted silver ran between her fingers and dropped into the blue water of the lake. She watched the silver droplets fall through the dark depths of the lake until they disappeared.

And then she saw something else in the water— her true reflection. A strong, confident girl who had faced her dark half and *won*.

❦ Chapter Thirty-Two

When Cassidy joined James back on the shore, she tried to read his face. *For once he doesn't look bored out of his head!* she thought.

"Okay, I don't think I can even begin to understand how you just did . . . well, any of it," he said. "But I'm really glad I was here to see it."

Cassidy shrugged. "You kind of started it, you know? I mean, I'm guessing that whole argument we had was a trick, right? To lure the evil twin out by making me mad?"

"Yeah, well . . . the plan didn't exactly go the way I thought it would. The demon was supposed to come after me, and then I figured while I distracted it, you could take over and cream it."

Cassidy wasn't sure what she should say next. James had seen and *heard* a lot. But she had to say something, something honest and real.

"James, I guess you've figured out that maybe some of that stuff—I mean, some of the things the dark half, *my* dark half, said were true."

He looked at her and then looked away. *Is he embarrassed?* "You don't have to say anything, Cass. Sometimes . . . well . . . you know . . ."

But he couldn't finish. Instead he reached out and touched the sleeve of her sweater that gaped from the slice of the bronze sword. "Are you okay?"

Cassidy knew that it would be healed even before she looked—but she pulled the flap of fabric away and let James see the thin pink line that would probably be gone by tomorrow.

"That's . . . amazing," he said. "How did you heal so fast?"

And somehow Cassidy knew that James wasn't ready to talk about what the dark twin had said. Not that Cassidy was, either. In fact, she hoped they could just both forget it ever happened. Unfortunately, she knew it probably wouldn't be all that simple.

"I guess I should go," James said. "I told Majesta I'd stop by . . ."

At those words, Cassidy waited for the prickly feelings of jealousy to poke at her spine and anger her—but not this time.

"Do you think she'd mind if I came along?" Cassidy asked. "I really want to tell her how sorry I am that she got hurt. I don't know if she'll ever forgive me, but I need to talk to her. I feel terrible that she got mixed up in this."

James smiled at Cassidy. "Yeah, I think she'd like that."

๑๑๑๑๑

Majesta smiled when she opened the door and saw James—but the smile vanished when she noticed Cassidy standing next to him. Majesta's left wrist was wrapped in a bandage, but other than that, she looked as stunning as ever.

"What are you doing here?" she asked Cassidy. "You want to knock me down again? Haven't you done enough?"

"She wants to talk to you, Majesta," James said. "Will you just listen to her, please?"

Cassidy saw that Majesta was pretty much helpless when James flashed the smile. She motioned for both of them to come inside.

It wasn't easy, but with James's help, Cassidy began trying to convince Majesta that she hadn't meant to hurt her and that she was truly sorry for what had happened.

"I guess I just opened the door really fast—I

didn't know you were there," Cassidy said. "And I didn't know you were hurt. I feel awful. I'll do anything to make it up to you, Majesta. I'm so sorry this happened."

The more Cassidy talked, the more she sensed that Majesta wished Cassidy would just leave so that she could be alone with James. She wondered if there was *anything* she could say that would make Majesta believe her. Cassidy doubted it, but at least she had tried. With some reluctance, Cassidy left Majesta and James together and started home. She didn't really have a choice. And she needed to make one stop along the way.

⌒⌒⌒⌒⌒

Luis's brother answered the door and pointed Cassidy toward the family room, where she found Luis battling video demons on a large-screen television. Cassidy thought about the demon—her *own evil twin demon* that she'd just defeated—and felt the gap widen between herself and the normal life she used to have.

"Hey," she said. Luis looked up but then quickly looked back to the bloody battle taking place on the screen.

"What?" he said.

"Can we talk?" Cassidy asked.

"Sure, talk," Luis said, then punched the hand control with his thumb, unleashing a series of violent strikes that obliterated a hideously shaped monster.

"Um, could you stop that for just a minute, please? I really need you to listen."

Luis paused the game. The hero, a buff, dark-haired fighter, stood in midstrike—his face in a fierce grimace as he faced a winged dragon with razor-sharp claws.

"I just talked to Majesta," Cassidy said, glad to have Luis's attention at last. "I explained what happened, and I told her that I was sorry. Anyway, I guess she *sort of* understands." Cassidy waited for Luis to respond, but he didn't.

"I just wanted to tell you that I really didn't know she fell," Cassidy continued. "I know what you saw, but it wasn't the way it looked."

"Well, it looked like you opened the door and pushed her down the steps and then went back inside."

"I know, Luis. I *know* that's what it looked like—but that's not what happened."

"You don't like Majesta," Luis said. "That's no secret."

"That's not—" Cassidy wanted to say, *That's not true*—but it was true—at least in part. "Honestly, Luis, Majesta hasn't always been my favorite person. I guess I've always been kind of jealous of her. But I never wanted to hurt her."

"I don't get it, Cass," Luis said. "I can't understand why you'd be jealous."

"Majesta's kind of perfect, Luis, or haven't you noticed? Perfect looks, perfect body, perfect clothes—and yeah, okay, it's embarrassing, but I guess I've sort of had a crush on James, and it looks like those two are—you know—together."

"You really think Majesta's perfect?" Luis asked. "She's got, like, zero sense of humor. And have you noticed how much goes over her head—like . . . *whoosh*!" Luis ran his hand over the top of his head to demonstrate, and Cassidy laughed.

"I didn't mean to hurt her, Luis," she repeated. "Do you believe me? It's really important that you believe me."

Luis nodded. "Yeah, I guess. I mean, I know you're not that way."

Cassidy thought about what Luis said. *The only reason I'm "not that way" is because I keep the dark thoughts under control,* she realized. The dark thoughts would always be there. It was only when they were unleashed that they had the power to cause problems—to cause pain. She was glad that Luis was her friend again . . . and wondered if she would ever be able to say the same about Eliza.

Luis handed Cassidy one of his controls. "Hey, want to play this new game with me? There's, like, this set of demons you have to fight, and each one is ten times worse than the one before."

"Sorry, Luis," Cassidy said, handing the control back to him. "I've got to get home or the demon called my *mom* is gonna come after me."

☙☙☙☙☙

Before going to bed that night, Cassidy opened the box of coins and took out the fourth coin. It was, as she expected, warm to the touch. She studied the image of the woman with the sword. She looked closely at the woman's face—only half of her face was showing; the other half was hidden behind the blade of the sword. But the part of the woman's face that was visible was strong, confident, and utterly calm. *A warrior,* Cassidy realized.

She fell asleep holding the coin. Sometime in the night she awoke. The coin had become hot and had left an imprint on the palm of her hand. She dropped the coin onto her blanket but in the darkened room saw that the skin on her hand continued to glow.

Then a brighter light appeared in her room. Once Cassidy's eyes adjusted, she saw her ancestors Ng Mui and Wing Chun standing at the foot of her bed. They smiled at Cassidy, and their warmth filled the room.

"Daughter of Light, you've come so far," said Ng Mui. She was dressed in her traditional tunic and trousers of tangerine silk. Beside her, Wing Chun was dressed in apricot silk.

"You are becoming a true warrior princess now," said Wing Chun. *"You know that, don't you? You feel it?"*

Cassidy rubbed the circular impression in the middle of her palm. It was beginning to fade, but she could still feel it. She wondered if it would always be a part of her now.

"Each of us holds both dark and light within us. Your mirror image was the dark side of your spirit, and you faced it—and defeated it," said Ng Mui.

"This is your gift, Mingmei, and it is the most precious gift of all because it is within you," said Wing Chun. *"You hold the power to control any dark thoughts that threaten you. These are demons of the mind, and they are most powerful."*

"They will always be with you," said Ng Mui. *"They never go away, and they must always be fought. It's not always easy—the darkness can be very tricky. Sometimes it masks itself as light."*

Chapter Thirty-Three

Cassidy hadn't heard from James in a while. She had forced herself to call him before school the next day, just to see if things were normal, but he hadn't answered. Or called back.

Well, unless he drops out of Wing Chun, I'm going to have to deal, she told herself. *Because there's no way I'm going to stop training.*

It was weird, not hearing from him all day, not speaking to him.

Maybe James wasn't the ally promised by her ancestors after all. Maybe that was just wishful thinking on her part. Maybe she just *wanted* him to be the ally so that they could spend more time together.

She had been able to fight her dark half by using a drill she'd learned from Master Lau—by closing her eyes and finding that calm center. *What if Master Lau's my true ally?* she wondered as she headed for the Happy Bunny after school. *What if he's the one who's supposed to guide me and help me prepare for whatever it is I'm supposed to do? Doesn't that make more sense? Master Lau's a wise and experienced adult—and James is . . . well, James is just a kid, really. He could get hurt, and it would be my fault for thinking that he was my ally and involving him in all this!*

Cassidy decided to act right away, before she had time to change her mind. So she jumped on a bus and headed to Master Lau's studio. She didn't know if he would be there, but she had to try to see him. *I'll talk to him. I'll tell him about the coins—the demons—all of it. Even if he's not my ally, he'll understand. He's my teacher, and he'll help me.*

☙☙☙☙☙

The lights were out in the gym, but Master Lau's office glowed with a warm light. Cassidy walked toward the office and noticed that the door was open several inches.

Instead of the bright overhead light in the office, Cassidy saw that Master Lau had lit several candles. Incense burned in small brass containers and filled the air with a sickly sweet odor that Cassidy recognized even before she reached the door. Rotting fruit. She saw Master Lau dressed in a long dark robe standing before an altar made of black stone. He held something in one hand and dripped oil onto a burning candle with the other.

What's he doing? Cassidy wondered. The candle and the oil reminded her of the ceremony he performed on Eliza to call on the dark spirit to leave her body. She realized that he didn't know she was there, standing just outside the partially open door. Suddenly she felt uneasy and started to turn to leave when she sensed that Master Lau wasn't alone in the small room.

Cassidy stifled a gasp as she watched a cloud of smoky gray spirits rise up out of the flame. As he poured more oil from the small bottle onto the candle, spirit after dark spirit formed and joined the others that swirled around the room. Each spirit was like a malformed beast, and their hideously shaped mouths opened in silent screams as they circled the small room. They looked as if they were in agony, with horrible tortured expressions on their faces.

Cassidy felt a chill that seemed to go straight to her marrow. Master Lau was calling up dark spirits from some awful place that she couldn't even imagine. She had to get out of there, but she felt rooted to the spot outside her teacher's door by a terror that gripped her throat.

I have to be calm, she realized. *I can't let him find me here!* She concentrated on visualizing a clear, sparkling pool, on following her breath until she felt her racing heart slow to its normal, even rhythm. Then she slipped away from the door quickly and without a sound.

Moments later Cassidy stood on the sidewalk and looked back toward the dark building where the terrifying ceremony was taking place.

Ng Mui's words echoed in her mind: *"The darkness sometimes masks itself as light."* Cassidy swallowed hard as she realized the horrible truth. Her teacher, her beloved Master Lau, was not what he appeared to be.

ᏩᏩᏩᏩᏩ

The bus ride home seemed never-ending. The entire trip, Cassidy replayed the scene in her mind—hoping, praying that she'd missed something, that it was only her imagination, that it only *looked* as if Master Lau had been calling up evil spirits. But Cassidy couldn't ignore the truth, and she was sure that what she saw had been real.

She felt nauseated at the thought of how close she'd come to telling Master Lau everything. She'd been ready to ask for his help—and he was drawing on the darkest energies of all. *What*, she wondered, *was he doing with those dark spirits?*

She remembered the awful smell in the *shifu's* office—the smell of rotting fruit—overripe peaches—the same smell that was in her room after the burglary.

Was it Master Lau? Did he break into the house to steal the coins, or was he after something else? My laptop? My mother's silver?

None of it made sense—but Cassidy had the nagging feeling that she was missing something. *What is it? I saw something in his office that was just . . . not supposed to be there . . . something that I tried to ignore.*

Cassidy pictured the scene again—*Master Lau was dressed in a long robe, and he was dripping the sickeningly sweet oil onto the candle.* But he was holding something else in his other hand. Cassidy closed her eyes and forced herself to remember what it was . . . *He was holding a photograph in his other hand—the photograph of my grandfather!*

Chapter Thirty-Four

"Did you forget?" Wendy asked when Cassidy walked into the kitchen. She pointed to the Happy Bunny work schedule posted on the refrigerator.

"Oh my God, I did forget. Mom, I'm sorry," Cassidy said. "I missed the first bus, and then the second one was late—I was supposed to do cleanup tonight, right?"

"Right, and this isn't the first time you've missed cleanup lately," Wendy said. "I thought you were trying to save for those jeans. Cass, you're not being very responsible."

Cassidy couldn't believe what she was hearing.

How am I supposed to do this? her thoughts screamed inside her. *I just saw my teacher calling up evil spirits, and now my mom's on my case about the Happy Bunny schedule! And I can't even tell her what's going on—I can't tell anybody! Not James. Not Eliza. No one.*

"It's too much!" Cassidy said out loud, and bolted up to her room. She glanced around for Monty, but he was making himself scarce.

Cassidy had never felt so alone. The gap that she felt between herself and the normal world had been growing. It was so wide now that it was as if she couldn't even *see* familiar faces on the other side. Eliza wasn't her friend anymore—and who could blame her after what happened with the fox demon? Luis would always be Luis—a wonderful friend, fighting video demons from the safety of his family room.

Her parents would always love and support her, but they could never understand what was happening. What would they do—*ground her* to keep her safe from the demons? And the other adult she would have once turned to was Master Lau, who might now be the very last person in the world she could trust.

Cassidy paced her room. She was supposed to be downstairs, helping her mother prepare dinner, but there was no way she could face anyone right now. She was too angry, too upset, too disappointed, too—

She caught sight of herself in the mirror.

A calm spirit—I'm supposed to find my calm spirit. But she saw nothing but turmoil on the face of the girl in the mirror. "You're no warrior!" she said to her reflection. "A warrior princess, ha! You've been fooling yourself all along. You mean nothing. The coins mean nothing. I quit!" She said the words again. "I quit! I'm giving Master Lau the coins. Let him do whatever he wants with them—I don't care anymore!"

She stared into the mirror, and then, almost as if her own reflection shamed her, she closed her eyes. She saw a dark pool of water, churning and turbulent with her troubled thoughts. *What happened to the clear, calm pool? Why can't I get that back?* As soon as she thought the words—she realized she knew the answer. *It's up to me,* she said to herself. *I can feel scared and alone and just give up—or I can face this myself. I have a choice.*

Swallowing hard, Cassidy forced herself to open her eyes—to face the darkness that she saw in the mirror. *I can do this,* she told herself. *I have control over my emotions. A true warrior faces the darkness within.* She felt her strength returning, and she repeated the words with conviction: "A true warrior faces the darkness within."

As Cassidy looked into the mirror, her image began to change. She saw that she was now dressed in a gorgeous robe of gold and jade brocade. Her face looked sure and strong, but more than anything, she looked calm. She felt the center of her right palm grow warm, and she held it up. In a small but perfect circle, she saw a faint image of the engraving from the coin imprinted there.

Cassidy knew at once that she was seeing her future self in the mirror—the true warrior princess—the person she was destined to become.

The reflection spoke to her: *"Mingmei, you know now that you must fight. You have earned this robe of gold and jade. Jade is an eternal symbol of power, but power born of both heart and mind. Gold represents purity of purpose. In gold and jade, Mingmei, you will do what is right.*

"You've faced the darkness within, but there is more. The vengeful spirits are hungry. Do you know what that means? You must fight them or they will devour us all—your past and your future. This is your destiny, a path through both shadows and light."

Cassidy felt an ache in her heart as tears stung her eyes. "I understand," she said. "I know this is my destiny, but I feel so alone. I don't know who to talk to anymore—I don't even know who I can trust!"

"You are not alone, Mingmei. Your grandfather is alive."

Cassidy gasped. "My grandfather? Alive?"

Her father had said that her grandfather had died in a boating accident but that they never found his body. She pictured the man with the white streak in his hair who gave her the coins. "How? Where?" Cassidy needed answers. "Is he here in Seattle? Is he in Hong Kong? I want to see him!"

"You'll see him in time, Mingmei. He's been watching out for you."

✿ Chapter Thirty-Five

All of Seattle's schools were closed the third week in March for teacher training, and Cassidy spent every day working at the Happy Bunny. On Friday the last child was picked up early, and Cassidy's mother told her that she could leave, too.

"Don't you need me to stay and clean up?" Cassidy asked.

"No, honey, you've been great this week," her mother said. "You've more than earned enough to buy whatever jeans you want. But for now, go, have fun, meet friends—do something different."

What friends? Cassidy thought, feeling a pang

of loneliness.

But the moment she stepped outside, Cassidy had a revelation. If she was strong enough to fight demons, she was strong enough to fight for her friendship with Eliza. So she clicked open her cell phone and hit Eliza's number on speed dial.

"Hey," said Eliza as she picked up the phone. To say that she sounded less than enthused would be an understatement. This was going to be more difficult than Cassidy thought.

"Hey," said Cassidy, and then there was a giant pause as Cassidy considered her next move. "Eliza, I get why you're not speaking to me," Cassidy said, almost involuntarily—as if the words were coming out of her mouth of their own volition. "I understand. Really. And I'm sorry for dragging you into my drama. You didn't deserve that. But I really miss you. Life's just not the same without my multicolor-haired friend. Can we be friends again?"

"I guess," Eliza said, still lacking the amount of enthusiasm Cassidy would have hoped for. Still, Cassidy could hardly contain her excitement.

"That's awesome! So, do you think . . . do you think maybe we can go back to the way we were?" Cassidy asked.

There was a long silence on the other end of the line. "I don't know," Eliza admitted. "I mean, things would have to be different than they were toward the end. But maybe we can hang out some?"

"That works!" Cassidy said.

"For me, too. But just you and me. No demons, no monsters, no craziness."

Cassidy laughed. "I'll do my best."

"Cool. So, how about tomorrow? I saw some awesome shoes on sale."

"Tomorrow's good." Cassidy ended the conversation and slipped the phone into her pocket, feeling lighter than she had in days. Then she headed toward the abandoned playground.

☙☙☙☙☙

A light dusting of snow covered the trees and all the playground equipment, muting the colors and softening the sharp edges of the empty apartment buildings. Cassidy felt enclosed in a cocoon of blanket softness—*A perfect place to train,* she thought.

After discovering that Master Lau was involved in something wrong—conjuring evil spirits or whatever he had been doing—Cassidy had considered quitting or finding another kung fu school. But one thing stopped her—the promise of Hong Kong. So she resolved that despite everything she'd seen, she would continue classes with Master Lau.

At least now she knew how to keep her emotions in check and concentrate on what she had to do. Since the day on the lake when she had fought her dark half, Cassidy had found it much easier to control any negative thoughts that arose. This, she realized, had been the gift for defeating the demon inside her. She had been given the calm mind of a warrior.

As Cassidy shed her fleece jacket and began a series of warm-up stretches, she thought about how much she had trusted Master Lau, and shuddered. He had seemed surprised at her skills during the private lessons. Had he been sizing up her abilities? But for what purpose? From now on, she knew, she would have to be careful around him, at least until she could figure out what he was up to. It was funny that James had seen through him from the start. When the time was right, she would talk to James about what she knew.

In the meantime, she'd continue to attend Master Lau's classes, but *this* would be her real training ground. And her teachers, Ng Mui and Wing Chun, would teach her everything she needed to know. Their words—their wisdom—would guide her.

Cassidy looked over at a tall pole that had once been part of a tetherball game. She ran toward the pole, leaping high, climbing the air, landing perfectly, soundlessly, effortlessly at the top. "Just like a real warrior princess," she said aloud, her words frosting the air.

She lifted her face to the gray sky and closed her eyes, imagining herself dressed in a robe of gold and jade—*jade, the eternal symbol of power, and gold, representing purity of purpose—pure heart, mind, and spirit.*

She felt the gentle touch of the cold snow on her face and marveled at how absolutely pure it felt against her warm skin. *In gold and jade you will do what is right.*

She smiled and stretched both arms out wide as the last snow of the season began falling around her, dusting her dark hair with its feather-soft flakes. *Say it*—she heard the words in her head—the words of her ancestors encouraging her—*say it.* And so she did.

"*I am Mingmei!*"